# One

*North Waltham, 1942*

'It never ceases to amaze me the way those two women get on.' Lucy Cadman's remark was directed at her husband Joe.

'I agree, love,' he quickly answered as he came to stand beside his wife. 'I have never known either one of them to say a bad word against the other. Theirs must be a friendship made in heaven.'

Mr and Mrs Cadman had run the local village shop for more years than they cared to remember. Their stock consisted of anything and everything, with home-made boiled sweets being their speciality. From behind the counter they were both watching Emma Pearson and Agnes Brownlow gaze at their half-empty shelves. It was now three years since Neville Chamberlain had announced that England was at war with Germany, and the shortage of food was

5

beginning to tell. Though the inhabitants of North Waltham would be the first to admit that because of this beautiful village, which was set in the heart of Hampshire, they fared a darn sight better than folk who lived in the big cities.

'What's the matter? Can't find anything to tempt you, Mrs Brownlow?' Joe Cadman asked, glancing at her with concern.

She turned her head and answered with a smile. 'Well, at least you've got some tins of Spam and there is quite a lot one can do with slices of Spam, though it wouldn't have been my first choice.'

Agnes Brownlow, known to her friends as Aggie, was hardly ever heard to complain though most would agree she had cause enough. Her husband had died in 1928, killed in a farming accident. She had been left with three children, two boys, Sidney and Lenny, who at the time had been aged seven and six, and a baby daughter Mary who had been only a few months old. The fact that she had survived so well was down to the fact that her brother John and his wife Mary both worked on what was the largest farm in Waltham. John was a life-saver to Aggie, keeping her supplied with fresh vegetables, rabbits and even the odd chicken.

John and Mary were housed in a tied cottage and that fact entitled them to a daily ration of free milk which they generously shared with John's sister and her family. Although her children had been deprived of their father, Aggie would readily agree they had never known what it was like to have to go without a good meal, and a further blessing was that living in this village they were surrounded by folk that cared for them and loved them dearly.

'Good Lord!' It was Emma Pearson who was exclaiming so loudly. 'A jar of Colman's Mustard! Long time since I've seen that on your shelves, Mr Cadman. My Sam will be made up when I take his sandwiches down at lunch time; he'll have mustard on almost any kind of sandwich you care to name.'

'Well, I'm glad you're pleased, Mrs Pearson. I must say I was when the wholesaler offered it to me. A bit further along on that same shelf you will find some bottles of Daddies Sauce if you're interested.'

'I most certainly am. My boys will go barmy when I offer them brown sauce to go with their sausages,' Aggie declared, laughing loudly.

Emma's husband Sam was the local blacksmith, a big burly man who looked tough enough to rip a man's head from his shoulders yet was really as gentle as a lamb. There hadn't been much to be thankful for since the start of this awful war but the Pearsons counted as the biggest blessing of all the fact that their youngest, Arabella, known mostly as Bella, had not been dragged away to do war-work. She had been conscripted into becoming a land girl and had been lucky enough to be assigned to Joe Briggs on a local farm which meant that most nights she managed to get home to sleep in her own bed.

On the other hand Emily, now twenty-two years old, just eleven months older than her sister Bella, was serving in the ATS, stationed in London at the moment, part of a motor pool, which meant she was chauffeuring bigwigs around the city. Emma's constant fear was for her daughter's safety. Already whilst driving she had been caught up in an air raid. A bomb had exploded only a few yards in front of her car and Emily had been injured. It was not so much that she had broken a leg and sprained her wrist that worried Emma but her daughter's traumatic experience of having to be dug out from a deep crater formed from the bomb blast, the memory of which would possibly haunt her for a long time to come. It seemed that you didn't have to be on a battlefield to be in the thick of this ghastly war. The citizens of London were experiencing the worst that the Luftwaffe could do.

Suddenly Emma felt incredibly weary, anxious to get home and prepare Sam's lunch. She would enjoy the walk to the smithy and she thought she might stay there with him for a while. Adding a bag of self-raising flour to the items she had already placed on the counter, she said, 'I think that's all I need for today, thank you, Mr Cadman.'

Joe Cadman reached beneath the counter and came up with two Rowntree's Table Jellies and two packets of Brown and Poulson's strawberry-flavoured blancmange powder.

'One of each for the pair of you,' he said, happy to see their eyes light up. 'I think I have enough to go around amongst my regular customers.' He beamed.

'Marvellous, ain't it?' Aggie grinned. 'We get so much pleasure from little things these days, don't we?'

'Course we do,' Emma happily agreed. 'Jelly and blancmange – me and Sam will have a bit of a party.'

Joe totted up the cost of their purchases, and having paid him they said their good-byes, linked arms and set off to walk home. Agnes's house was in the first cobbled street that they came to, and they hugged each other saying, 'See you tomorrow.'

Emma walked on. Her house was the very last at the far end of the next cobbled street. Opening the side gate she went down the path and opened the back door which opened directly into the scullery which in turn led into the big kitchen used mainly as the family living room. Dumping her shopping bags down Emma did as she always did, and went through the passageway to see if there was any post lying on the doormat. There was. Just one letter. Turning it over in her hands and glancing at the big bold writing she knew at once it was from their Tom. Oh, how her heart gladdened – that boy could put a smile on her face just thinking about him. He was truly a godsend, and he had come into their lives solely because of an organization known as the Toc H.

In the year of 1930, this quiet village had been altered considerably by the arrival of two coach loads of orphaned children, most of whom had never known their parents. Brought up in an institution, they had never known the love of a close family.

They were given two weeks' holiday, which had been organized and paid for by a team of men who were Toc H Society members, who had made themselves benefactors to underprivileged children. Families in the village had been approached and asked whether they were willing to offer hospitality to any of these children. Emma had discussed the matter at great length with her husband Sam, and they had agreed to take two children. For herself, she hadn't been too bothered as to whether they were boys or girls but Sam had been all for having boys.

The Reverend Michael Coyle, the rector of their local church, had encouraged local families to open their homes to these young children who had mainly spent their young lives shut away in institutions. Michael Coyle was a big man, very attractive, with deep dark-brown eyes and thick brown hair, who had time for others, time to listen and would always help to the best of his ability. Yet he himself had suffered a great tragedy. Years ago, a lorry had taken a sharp bend in the road far too quickly, mounted the pavement and his wife, together with their two young sons were all crushed against the side of the village pub. After the accident Michael had left the village for six months, staying at a retreat, but he had come back saying that this was where his family were buried and this was where his life's work was.

Sam had been delighted on being told that Tom Yates, who was nine years old, and John Kirby who was ten, had been assigned to their care for fourteen days. Even now, after all that had happened, Emma could recall their arrival in the utmost detail. The boys' hair had been cut so close it was almost as if their heads had been shaved. They had each been wearing short trousers which at their age was just not right. On top of which they were wearing nothing more than ragged shirts, the sleeves of which had been rolled up above their elbows showing really skinny arms. They had hardly any belongings except what they stood up in. The boys had been tongue-tied and wary, and Emma had been terrified, not knowing how to deal with them.

It was Sam who had saved the day! He had looked after the boys and he'd seen to it that they were suitably clothed. Where he had acquired so much underwear, so many shirts, jumpers and trousers, Emma hadn't dared to ask. She was aware that he had gone and bought both lads a brand new pair of lace-up shoes because he had been appalled at the state of their feet due to the fact that they were wearing shoes that were too small. Emma felt she had played her part by seeing that the boys were well fed.

The two weeks had not passed without incidents, some good, some bad. On the whole, though, it had been a miraculous experience for everyone concerned. By the final week Emma felt there was nothing that she wouldn't do to better the lives of these two lads. She was even telling herself that the addition of two boys to their family would be a marvellous thing. The two London boys and her own two girls were all getting on so well. However, all good things have to come to an end; but the whole family had admitted that they dreaded to think what kind of a life John and Tom would return to.

Michael Coyle was travelling on the coach with the children going back to London. His aim was to see for himself how the institute was run and to find out if he was able to help out in any way in the future. He had asked Sam to accompany him.

There had been no flag waving or cheering as the children waited to board the coaches. The air was filled with emotion. Not a soul could have predicted the difference in these children these past fourteen days had made. The good country air and the home cooking the villagers had provided had paid off, not to mention the fact that each and every child had received some new clothes to wear which had gone a long way to boosting their confidence.

Emma had linked her arm through her husband's as she watched her two tearful girls say their goodbyes to John and Tom. It was amazing, the bond that had sprung up between these children in such a short space of time.

'Tom doesn't like it in that home, so why can't they stay here with us?' Bella had asked, staring up at her father, her voice trembling, her eyes brimming with unshed tears.

'John would like to stay here too,' Emily had quietly added. 'He said he would get a job on one of the farms and pay you for his keep. Dad, would that be possible?'

Sam had looked at her with his heart in his mouth and all he had been able to mutter was, 'Talk about tugging at one's heart strings.' It had taken a moment for their father to compose an answer. He had bent low, placing his arms around his two girls to draw them close to his side.

'Your mother and I feel just the same way as you two do. We would dearly love to keep both boys here permanently, if only it was possible, and I am going to make some inquiries to see how I would have to go about it. But, for the time being all these children come under the control of the London County Council.'

'Well, it's not fair,' Bella cried loudly. 'If nobody wants them why can't they stay with us?'

For once in his life Sam had felt that he was out of his depth. He'd gently pushed Emily towards her mother and had wrapped his arms around Bella; holding her close he had whispered against her thick shiny hair, telling her that nobody had ever promised that life was going to be fair. He had also told her that he was going to do the best he could for the boys and vowed that they would never lose touch with either of them, no matter what.

When the order to board the coaches had been given, John had solemnly held out his hand to Emma.

'Oh, no, my lad, you don't get away from me as easily as all that,' she'd told him, forcing back her own tears and doing her best to smile. She had tugged him to her and enfolded him in her brawny arms, holding him close for a full minute before she rested her cheek against the top of his head. Then finally letting go of him she'd said, 'Don't for one moment think this is the last you will see of me. I will write to you and you must do your best to write to all of us. You will, won't you, John?'

Poor lad, he had been choked to his high teeth, so that all he could do was nod as he turned his back to her and let Sam lift him up into the coach.

Tom had been a very different kettle of fish. She had held him close and ruffled his hair before saying, 'You're a deep one, you are, Tom. You don't let your right hand know what your left hand is up to.'

Tom had leant his head backwards and stared up at her and to say that she had been surprised would have been putting it mildly, but there had been no mistaking that the big brown eyes of this rough and ready Cockney lad had been glistening as a slow trickle of tears overflowed and ran down his cheeks.

'You're not the hard nut you'd have us all believe, are you?' she'd murmured, the lump in her throat nearly choking her as she'd realized his skinny little body was trembling from head to foot.

In the end it had been Sam that had released her hold on Tom but as she had let him go he had said, 'Goodbye, Auntie Em, I'm gonna miss you.'

As Emma recalled that heart-breaking morning she freely admitted to herself that Sam had kept his word over the years, plodding through miles of red tape and battling against a great many officials who hadn't thought it was part of their job to be kind or caring.

# Two

Emma wasn't the only one who sometimes allowed her thoughts to wander down memory lane. Sam Pearson often looked back to that year. Innocent young lads and lasses of that era were now serving in the Armed Forces or were employed on important and often very dangerous war work.

Getting to know John Kirby and Tom Yates that year had made him realize that they were able to give their own daughters so many privileges that these boys could only dream of. When he had travelled to London with the Reverend Michael Coyle the sights that had met them had been utterly appalling. Total confusion and sheer pandemonium!

Soon after the children's holiday the London institution was closed and they were meant to move to Kent. As bad as the place might have been, it was to most of the children the only home they had ever known. Any small possessions they might have acquired were all inside that big grey building which stood alongside the Docks. Despite adults giving lengthy assurances the children were afraid. To them it was like going off into the unknown.

During the chaos, Tom Yates and John Kirby had gone missing. The weeks that had followed had been very distressing. So many people, including the police, had been involved but neither hide nor hair had been seen of the two young lads. The knowledge that they had no money and no one to turn to had almost driven Emma mad. For five long months she and Sam had had to cope with the continual questions their daughters asked. How could they answer them when they themselves had no idea how, where or why John and Tom had disappeared?

Then one dark evening there was a gentle knock on their back door. Two skinny scruffy-looking lads had appeared, but just the very look of them had been enough to make angels cry!

'Don't suppose you're pleased t'see us but we don't know where else t'go.' Those few words which had been muttered by John were imprinted for ever in his mind. Tom had looked the worse of the two. Ragged, under-nourished and dirty, he'd borne no resemblance to the self-assured lad that had left here five months ago. While Sam helped to clean them up Emma had set to and produced bowls of steaming hot thick soup and hunks of crusty bread. Emily and Bella had gone wild with delight when they had arrived home to find them there. 'Now they can stay with us for ever,' Bella had stated it as if it was a foregone conclusion, not a question.

Even now, all these years later, Sam shuddered as he recalled the rigmarole and all the red tape they had had to endure to even be allowed to keep in touch with the boys.

One of the saddest aspects of their return had been Tom's illness. The doctors had soon diagnosed that Tom had pleurisy, and had feared it could even be tuberculosis. The authorities had insisted that he be carted off to the Brompton Hospital in Chelsea, in south-west London. The obvious solution, and everyone's dearest wish, was that John should stay with the Pearson family, but despite all Sam's efforts it wasn't to be. It had felt as if he were knocking his head against a brick wall – so many rules and regulations! He had fought tooth and nail trying to prove that he and Emma would be suitable parents if they were granted permission to adopt both boys. When that avenue had been closed they had literally begged to be allowed to be foster parents. But the answer had been the same: no.

In desperation he had contacted the City of London branch of the Toc H Society. With the backing of this organization he and Emma had been granted limited privileges. From that moment on regular contact with both boys had been assured and to all the residents of North Waltham Tom Yates and John Kirby were regarded as members of the Pearson family.

Then came the day when John had reached the age of fifteen and was turned away from the establishment to fend for himself. Naturally he had come home.

Sam paused in his reminiscences. What a day that had been! The women had shed buckets of tears, which hadn't made any sense because it was such a happy day; flags had been flying everywhere, and loads of balloons; even a brass band for John to march with through the lanes. Food and drink had appeared in abundance. Every inhabitant had turned out to welcome the lad home.

One year later they had done it all over again when Tom had returned home.

# Three

During the years that followed Emma had been happy beyond belief. Her every prayer had been answered. To all intents and purposes she and Sam now had two daughters and two sons. Whether or not Tom and John were legally part of their family now no longer mattered. They were where they were wanted and loved. She had watched the four of them grow into adults and she had become aware that Emily and John had deep feelings for each other.

The only shadow cast over everybody's life had been that the threat of a second war was looming. Then in September 1939 that threat had become a reality.

John had already volunteered for the armed forces and Tom too would have enlisted but he had worked at the Woolwich Arsenal from the day he was fifteen years old and his employment was classed as being of military importance. During wartime it was classed as a reserved occupation, which meant that not only could he not join any of the armed forces but he could not change his employment either.

For some time life seemed to carry on quite normally. Tom came home at regular intervals though during the weekdays he had been lucky enough to find lodgings with Daisy and Donald Gaskin. The Gaskins were true Londoners with a very large family, most of whom were married but still living close to their parents.

Daisy and Donald still occupied a large house in south London, which was within walking distance of Woolwich Arsenal. Tom had landed on his feet; the whole Gaskin family treated him as one of their own.

Sam and Emma had only met the Gaskins on one occasion yet they had been given such a warm welcome they had agreed they were true Cockneys but nevertheless they had hearts of gold.

The quiet phoney war continued over Christmas and well into the New Year. Then in the month of May 1940 something had happened which was beyond imagination! The British Expeditionary Force was stranded in France. Thousands of troops were pinned down in the outlying towns and villages of France. The carnage was beyond belief. The wounded and dying were everywhere.

A great evacuation had immediately been put into operation, and hundreds of boats of all shapes and sizes had set off from Portsmouth to attempt to get the wounded. A great many of the troops, who had become stranded on the beaches, were rescued and brought safely back to England's shores. For days, boats and ships, even very small craft, had repeatedly made journeys across the sea. The Luftwaffe had shown them no compassion. As the troops walked waist high into the sea in order to board any boat they could reach, bombs had rained down on them.

Small craft and large vessels had been sunk, just disappeared beneath the waves, which made it seem even more like a miracle when the Government announced that almost 340,000 British and French troops had been brought safely back to England.

Sadly, John Kirby, aged just twenty-two, had not been amongst that number. He had drowned.

The Pearson family had been devastated. Reverend Michael Coyle had later held a memorial service in Saint Michael's Church for John and it had seemed as if every single person living in North Waltham had turned out to attend. To know that John had been so well loved had gone a long way to easing Emma's and Sam heartbreak.

It was Emily that her parents worried over the most. She had been inconsolable.

# Four

After the death of John, summer had seemed a long time coming. The cold weather had seemed to drag on. It had been such a blow to lose John but it had been some consolation that the whole of the local community had shown that it considered John Kirby to be a son of Mr and Mrs Pearson, despite the fact they had never legally been allowed to adopt the boys.

Now that the first German daylight bombing raids on London had started, Emma feared even more for the safety of Emily and Tom. How in God's name had Emily ever got herself into the ATS, she often asked herself? What with the dangerous work that Tom was doing she felt that the pair of them were literally in the front line. It had been sometime since they had been able to come home at the same time.

The lovely memory of the last time they were home had kept Emma going for some while. It had been a great time for all of them although there had been tears mixed with the laughter. Like the morning when she had taken an early morning cup of tea up to her two girls. The bedroom door had been ajar and she had cautiously peeped in to see both girls huddled up in the one bed. Emily had been crying softly and Bella had been holding her close. Placing the cups down on to the floor Emma had made to go back downstairs but as the girls had begun to talk, her curiosity and concern had got the better of her and she had stayed and listened.

Poor dear Emily. She was confessing that with John gone she had lost so much and, more to the point, she felt that the rest of her life had been taken from her – there would be no marriage, no children.

Just listening had made Emma's heart ache and it hadn't helped when Bella too had started to cry and had said bitterly, 'Damn this bloody war.'

Tom was still the cheeky chappie he had always been, full of stories that concerned dodgy deals and the clothes that he wore! It was obvious he had no worries where clothing coupons were concerned. He was always well-dressed and at times, when it suited him, he would play the part of a dandy to a tee. Though, buried not too deeply, he still had vivid memories of his young days when the rule in the institution had been the survival of the fittest. With Tom for a friend you were set for life. Hurt him or any member of his family and he became an enemy.

He never tired of telling friends how great it felt to be a true member of a real family. To Tom, Sam and Emma were his parents in every sense of the word. He loved them both more dearly than words could ever say and wherever possible he made it his business to see that they wanted for nothing.

News from London was scarce and it was some time before Emma and Sam had learnt that their daughter Emily had been injured in an air raid. Again they had Tom to thank. He had borrowed a car, begged, borrowed or stolen some petrol, and turned up late at night and had left again by four the next morning because he dared not miss a shift at the Arsenal. He had come in person to re-assure them that Emily would be fine.

Apparently Emily had been almost home and dry when she had heard the wail of the air-raid siren and almost instantaneously had felt the car rock from side to side. A bomb had fallen approximately two hundred yards in front of the car she had been driving. Emily had had to be dug out from a deep crater caused by the blast of the bomb. Yet thankfully the only damage to her body had been a broken left leg and a badly sprained right wrist. Only time would tell what harm she had suffered mentally. Her forehead had been badly cut and her head injuries had concerned the doctors the most. Emily still needed to regain her confidence since the accident.

Trouble never comes in single portions.

During a really heavy air raid, whole streets of houses in the Woolwich area of London had been razed to the ground. Several members of the Gaskin family had lost their entire homes. Donald and Daisy Gaskin had learnt that their home had been declared unsafe to live in, but Mr Tomlinson, their landlord, had come up trumps by offering them a garden flat in Manor Street in Clapham. Daisy had moaned that it was on the south side of the River Thames, but Donald had quickly reminded her that there was a war going on and that beggars could not be choosers.

Seeing as how Tom was only their lodger the landlord was not legally bound to re-house him. However, Tom had never failed to produce a good bottle of Scotch whisky and a few cigars whenever Mr Tomlinson hinted that he was running short. London's code of honour demanded that favours be repaid. The flat offered to Mr and Mrs Gaskin had three bedrooms and Tom had been able to move with them.

It was a great relief to both Emma and Sam that Tom was able to meet up with Emily from time to time. When Emily had been caught up in that air raid she had been forced to spend a few days in a London hospital before being transferred to a military convalescent home down in Kent. It was during those first few days, when Emily had been feeling at her lowest, that Tom had taken Daisy Gaskin to the hospital to visit Emily. The outcome of that visit had been that the whole of the Gaskin family more or less adopted her. That had turned out to be no bad thing as Emily had cause to remember. Even being in the ATS, surrounded by women of all ages, she had soon found out that London was not only a dangerous place in time of war but it could also be a very lonely place.

Even back home in North Waltham things were beginning to change. Despite the abundance of local produce it had become a time of austerity and shortages. It was sad but true that even the village had changed. Lionel and Marion Trenfield, who owned the Big House and were always kindly thought of as lord and lady of the manor, had moved out of their home and were now living in a simple cottage that stood within the vast grounds that surrounded the house. Servicemen of many nationalities, Canadian, American and Australian, were now billeted in the house and troops were housed in quarters within the grounds. Two men from the British catering corps, Jimmy Thomas and Mick Meade, had been installed as chefs. Makeshift buildings had been erected on the edge of the woods. Rows of huts and one very large structure with a corrugated roof, presumably for use as a dining hall, plus a block of toilets and washing facilities, had practically sprung up and a battalion from the Royal Engineers had moved in. Yet none of the villagers were aware of what went on up there.

Those who had come were enough to make the social life a bit more lively, at least for the youngsters who were still living at home, including Bella, and of course the extra land girls who had been drafted in to work on the farms were more than glad of their company.

Emma shook her head and told herself to stop all this day-dreaming. If she were honest with herself she would admit that she was feeling jealous; it was a hard thing to admit but her nose had been well and truly put out. She glanced up to where Emily's letter, which had arrived a few days ago, was propped up behind the clock on the mantel-shelf. It was typewritten by one of the nurses because Emily's wrist had not yet healed properly. She didn't need to read it again; she knew every line off by heart. The gist of the letter was that Emily was being dis-charged from the military home and now, eight weeks after she had arrived there, she was to appear before a medical board in London and would then be granted a period of compassionate leave.

Wonderful! Our Emily will be coming home on leave! This had been her first re-action and she had danced around the kitchen. Then she'd read on. First off, Tom was taking her to stay a couple of days with Daisy and Donald Gaskin because it would be handy for the medical board, which was housed in Whitehall, and also he wanted to keep a promise which he had made to Emily a long time ago.

He was going to take Emily to Epsom Races!

Would you believe it? *Our Emily should be coming straight home to rest and be looked after by her own family,* Emma thought, feeling aggrieved. Not going to stay with folk she hardly knew and she certainly didn't need to be dragged off to see horses racing. God Almighty! She'd have something to say to Tom when he did finally bring their Emily home.

Sam was in her bad books as well as Tom because when he'd read the letter he had been smiling.

'What are you worrying yourself about?' he'd asked, with a big silly grin on his face. 'It will only be for a couple of days and then our Emily will spend the rest of her leave down here with us.'

'Yes, that's all very well but we don't know how long that leave will be yet, do we?' she had stormed back at him.

Emma knew she was being petty. Surely she should be feeling on top of the world. Emily, according to all the reports they had received, was making a remarkable recovery and she should be happy for her. Tom won't let the wind blow on her, she chided herself. She was sure they had had a wonderful day out together and she would see her daughter very soon.

At long last her usual sunny nature took over. It wasn't in her to stay cross with Tom or Sam for too long and she must on no account become possessive. I know what I'll do, she thought, I'll spend the whole afternoon baking so that when Sam arrives home and opens the door he will be met with the gorgeous smell of rabbit stew and dumplings, and I'll make a really deep apple pie.

You're not doing this for Sam, she rebuked herself; you're doing it to ease your own conscience. However, she was humming as she laid out her pastry board and rolling pin.

# Five

'You'd never believe there was a war going on,' Emily remarked to Tom as she stood by his side gazing out over the wonderful green turf of Epsom Racecourse. 'I still can't get my head around the fact that horse racing is still an ongoing event,' she muttered, more to herself than to Tom.

'My dear Emily, when will you learn that there is one law for the rich and another for the poor? Horse racing is the sport of kings. The little man in the street likes his flutter but that counts for nothing; it's money all the way along the line that keeps horse racing on the go.'

Tom had given her a searching look before he had spoken again and when he did his voice had held a very serious note. 'You may have discarded your crutches but you're not doing too well walking with a stick, so please be careful, take things slowly, I don't want you breaking your other leg.'

Emily smiled, the freedom of being here on this lovely sunny day was such a tonic and she was certain she hadn't felt so happy in a very long time. They had had a wonderful day but Emily was still slightly puzzled by the life Tom led in London, so she had to question him.

'You turned up in Kent yesterday, your mate drove you there in a van and you introduced him to me as Bert Fisher. I hadn't got a clue as to how you knew him or where he got the petrol from to be driving a van.'

Tom tried to speak but Emily had held up her hand.

'Please, Tom, let me get this sorted out in my head. Your mate drove us to Clapham, to where you are now living with Daisy and Donald. Donald immediately told me they were so pleased that I was going to stay a couple of nights with them. Daisy gave us a really good dinner and about half past eight we all walked up Manor Street to the pub. God knows how many of their family turned up but all of them were so kind to me, really concerned about my injuries, and we ended up having a great night.'

'Well, that's no bad thing, is it?' Tom interrupted her.

'No, as I said, it was great; everyone was singing all the old London songs with a few Irish ones thrown in for good measure. For a while I think we all forgot that there was a war going on. Thing is, I feel guilty because Daisy insisted that I share her big bed and I don't know where Donald slept.'

Tom was grinning like a Cheshire cat. 'There's no need for you to worry over Don, he's used to his family turning up and he's happy to doss down anywhere.'

'It seemed as if we had hardly closed our eyes when you were hollering at me to hurry up because we had to catch a bus. We made it to the Clapham Common tube station with time to spare.'

'We wouldn't 'ave if I hadn't dragged you out of Daisy's bed, you silly cow.'

'Tom! Don't you dare swear at me.'

'Oh, going all high and mighty now, are we? Sorry, but my name ain't Clive an' I don't 'appen to be a chinless wonder like that silly prat,' he said, raising his voice far more than was necessary.

Oh dear! Why the hell did Tom have to bring Clive Beaumont into the conversation? She dearly loved Tom, warts and all, he was smashing, always there for her, and she really did love the very bones of him. But he did get a bee in his bonnet when it came to Clive Beaumont.

She had first met Clive when she had drawn orders to drive for him. Her own impression of Captain Beaumont didn't really amount to much; he was too full of his own importance and he certainly fancied his luck where the ladies were concerned. Having said that, he always managed to look immaculate even when he was off duty and casually dressed.

From that first meeting he had seemed to turn up wherever she went and if she were truthful at times he had made a big impression on her. Whenever they had any free

36

time, which wasn't very often, she went dancing at the Rainbow Rooms in Piccadilly with three other recruits from the motor pool, and Clive Beaumont was the perfect partner on the dance floor even though he was a show-off on and off the floor. On only one occasion had Tom turned up in the Rainbow Rooms and of course it had to be an evening when Clive was there with some friends of his. She had needed no telling that Tom had disliked Clive on sight.

Looking at Emily's straight face Tom was immediately sorry that he had raised his voice to her. Holding out his hand to her he said, 'Come on let's make a move. I'll put my bets on and then I'll show you where the Tote is and tell you how it works. You can bet as little as two bob on the Tote.'

Two hours later Emily had gained confidence. Totting up her losses and gains she found she was better off by the princely sum of four pounds and six shillings. She had lost sight of Tom and when she did catch a glimpse of him he was surrounded by half a dozen men, all of whom were engrossed in their racing catalogue. As the day was drawing to an end she took her close-fitting hat off and ran her fingers through her long thick chestnut hair. It had been piled up under her hat, clipped in place on top of her head, but a few strands had come adrift, so she pulled them up using two side-combs which she took out of her handbag to secure them. She looked up and found Tom was within yards of her and had been closely watching her.

It sometimes surprised Emily how great the bond between herself and Tom was. How well she remembered when he and John had first come to stay with her mum and dad for a holiday. Both she and Bella had loved those two boys right from the very start. And the sadness she had felt during the time when both boys had sneaked away from the institution and had not been heard of for weeks on end! How tough it must have been for them, living rough all that time. Then the joy when they had turned up on the doorstep, and God alone knew from that day onwards how hard her parents had fought the authorities to be allowed to keep both boys. It had never happened. Not legally. Yet from that day they had never ever again lost touch. They had merged into the family as if they had been born to her parents and come the day when they were legally allowed to leave the institution they had lived and work-ed as members of the Pearson family. It had been by their own choice, which made them doubly precious.

Until this awful war had come about she had made up her mind that she was going to spend the whole of her life with John. She had learnt at least one thing; in this life nothing is for certain.

Tom had gone out of his way to give her a day at the races and she mustn't spoil it by dragging up the past. All the sorrow and the tears wouldn't alter anything.

Death was so final. At that point Tom turned and smiled at her. Only one thing was wrong and it worried her. Tom had just turned twenty-two, but he looked to be nearer thirty because his skin did not have a healthy glow. This problem, sad to say, stemmed from him working with ammunitions and coming into close contact with gunpowder. You did not have to be in the thick of the fighting to become a casualty in this war.

They made the last bus home. Emily arrived before Tom. The bus was full and the majority of the passengers were Tom's workmates. Seeing Emily arrive on her own, several females, both young and old, called out to her.

'You alright, luv? Tom in trouble, is he?'

'Caught passing dodgy fivers, and now he's banged up down at the local cop-shop – is that it?'

Just then the bus driver appeared. 'I'll give yer a lift up, my darling, when you're ready; bit of a high step, that is. And as for our Tom, it's more than likely he's won a hefty bundle an' had it away on his toes, an' if that is the case then Woolwich Arsenal won't be seeing his arse for dust.'

It had all been good-hearted fun and the driver, good as his word, practically lifted her up the steps and on to the bus while all the other passengers cheered loudly.

However, Emily heaved a heavy sigh of relief when Tom did finally get there. She was so exhausted that her head drooped, and Tom twisted round so that her head rested on his shoulder.

Lowering his voice to little more than a whisper, he said, 'I'd been given a tip for that last race, it was a rank outsider, but the odds were fantastic so I put something on for you. I want you to buy yourself something nice, and seeing as 'ow you're going to spend your compassionate leave at home with Mum and Dad and Bella you'll be able to use some of your winnings and give them a nice treat.'

Emily raised her eyes to meet his, and

softly asked, 'What have I ever done to deserve you?'

Tom waited to hear her breathing slow so he knew that Emily was asleep, and it was only then that he answered her question.

'You and yours took John and me in when no one else wanted to know. Your parents not only gave us both a home, they made us part of a family that loved and cared for us. And that, Emily my love, is something that all the money in the world couldn't buy. And when the war finally comes to an end it will be pay-back time and then I fully intend to do my best to care for our mum and dad and you and Bella and to ensure that none of you will ever want for anything.'

His vow had been made in such earnest that Emily would have needed no telling that he had meant every single word.

# Six

Emily slowly opened her eyes. For a while she struggled to remember where she was.

Everything was strange. The room, the noise that was coming in through the open window, the fact that she was in this big strange bed which had brass knobs on each corner of the bed-rails. She raised herself up on her elbows and shook her head quite hard, telling herself to get with it. This is the second night you've slept in this bed with Daisy, and Tom took you to Epsom Races yesterday. She lay still, feeling quite worried. How could she have forgotten where she was and how she had got here?

It was all becoming clear now and she allowed herself a wry smile.

No wonder her brain felt a bit muddled. She and Tom had arrived home yesterday evening just before eight o'clock. Straight off Tom had announced it was to be a fish supper for everyone. Following that merry meal they had all gone to the pub again. Tom had paid for everybody's supper and for all the drinks. He assured all and sundry that he had done well by placing his bets at the track.

For the second night running it had been a lively evening.

No wonder she had been tired out when she and Daisy had finally got to bed. It had been a long day and she knew she'd had more to drink than was good for her. Her tongue felt swollen, her mouth as dry as a bone. She threw back the bedclothes and looked at the small clock that was standing on top of a tall chest-of-drawers.

'Good God!' she exclaimed out loud. The hands of the clock showed it was a quarter to eleven. Where was everyone? How could she not have heard Daisy get up? How could they have let her sleep so long? What was all the noise about?

She walked to the window and flung back the thin curtains, remembering that Daisy had told her there were no black-out curtains in the bedrooms because there hadn't been time for her to make them.

The windows were already opened, Daisy must have seen to that when she got up. It was a brilliant sunny day here in Clapham. If she looked upwards it enabled her to get a good view. Kids were playing out in the street, women were sitting on their window sills, nattering away to their neighbours, old men were leaning against walls, some were huddled in a group noisily discussing today's newspapers.

Emily felt she would die if she didn't get a drink. Preferably a strong cup of hot tea. Please God don't let me find that Daisy's tea caddy is empty. She pulled her cotton dressing gown around her, pushed her feet into her slippers and reached for her stick that was leaning against the wall. As she opened the bedroom door she was thankful that this flat was semi-basement. At least it was all on one level. These houses were old Victorian ones, which had four floors, and most had been turned into flats many years ago. It had been a relief that Daisy and Donald had been given a flat with three bedrooms, not that the third bedroom was up to much; small in size, it was at the moment packed with whatever they had been able to salvage from their own home.

'Is anyone about?' Emily called loudly. Not a sound. The silence felt weird. Wherever the Gaskin family were there was always non-stop noise. She opened the back door. The garden – or was it just a yard? – was strewn with boxes of all shapes and sizes, pieces of furniture and what looked like several old carpets which were damp and mouldy.

'Anyone out here?' Emily called again, taking a few steps along the uneven pathway.

'Oh, you are up.'

The voice had made Emily jump but she relaxed as she turned her head to the left and saw just the head and shoulders of a woman appearing over the wooden fence.

'They've all gone out and I've been left in charge of you. Been round twice I 'ave but you were dead t'the world so I let yer be. Anyway, I'm Lucy Bannister, I live 'ere next door as yer can see. Don't know why I'm wasting me breath you can see for yerself where I live. I'll come round, got orders to make yer a bit of breakfast. Won't be two ticks.'

The head and shoulders disappeared and Emily went back indoors. She was thoroughly baffled again. Why would everyone disappear at the same time? She had only a minute to wait before the gate at the end of the garden opened and the friendly neighbour from next door stepped in.

'First bloody sunny day we get this year an' I'm stuck indoors,' she groaned to Emily as she undid the scarf that was tied round her head and started to remove the dinky curlers from her hair.

'Oh, please don't feel that you have to be responsible for me,' Emily told her firmly, 'but there is one thing I would like to know: where is everybody?'

'Well, don't go all shirty on me,' Lucy Bannister replied with a brief smile. 'First things first. Yer can 'ave a cat's lick for now an' put some clothes on while I make us both a nice cup o' tea an' then I'll start at the beginning and tell yer all yer need to know.'

Emily would dearly have loved to say, 'May we have the tea first and then I could maybe have a proper wash and get dressed?' Instead she just murmured, 'Thank you,' as she watched Lucy holding the kettle under the cold water tap. It wasn't long before Lucy brought a tray into Daisy's living room with two large breakfast cups of hot tea.

Emily lay back in her chair, her hands wrapped around the large cup; she had taken several sips, it was scalding hot but it tasted like the best cup of tea she had ever had.

'Are yer feelin' better now?' Lucy asked as Emily slowly began to really drink her tea.

'Yes, I am and the tea is really good; it was kind of you to come round. I feel so daft, sleeping half the morning away and then finding that everyone has gone out.'

'You were tired out,' Lucy told her. 'After all, from what I've bin told it ain't all that long since you was in yer car when it got blown down a bomb 'ole. You got t'take things easy for a bit. Finish yer tea an' then I'll make yer some toast – will that do yer t'be going on with?'

Emily nodded her head. 'You don't have to stay with me or wait on me, really, I can manage on my own. But I would like to know what has happened. I have this funny feeling that something has gone wrong or why else would everyone disappear at the same time?'

Lucy had picked the teapot up and taken it through into the scullery to pour more boiling water over the tealeaves. Emily could see her clearly, as she took off her wrap-around overall and ran her fingers through her thick mop of fair curly hair; those dinky curlers had certainly done their job. She looked quite presentable now in a navy blue dress that had a spray of pink flowers em-broidered across one shoulder. Emily thought that she would put Lucy's age at somewhere near forty, but then she had never been any good at guessing ages. Only trouble was the shabby slippers on Lucy's feet, but who had enough coupons to spare these days to enable them to buy slippers? It was hard enough to say that you owned one decent pair of shoes.

'Second cup?' Lucy asked, as she came back carrying the teapot.

'Yes, please,' Emily said, without any hesitation.

'Right, I've cut the bread. I only 'ave t'put it under the grill. I don't for one minute think Daisy 'as got any butter, but I know Tom brought her an enormous tin of marmalade which she split up into jars. Will some of that do?'

Emily found she was laughing, really laughing, and Lucy joined in with her. 'Yeah, I know exactly what you're thinking; this war has turned most of us into criminals but there again, from day t'day it's become a fight of the fittest and Gawd 'elp them that gets caught.' Lucy suddenly stopped talking and sighed deeply. 'I'm afraid Tessa, Daisy's eldest girl, has found that out.'

'Why, what's happened to Tessa?'

'Look, luv, they should be back soon an' I'd rather they told you themselves. Though while yer finishing that tea I may as well tell you – the bloody Germans are 'aving another go at the centre of London.'

'I already know that the air raids have started up again,' Emily replied quietly.

'No, luv, you don't know. This lot is different, started early yesterday morning, and they've already bin over this morning. Don't know where the name came from but already folk are calling them doodlebugs! Came crashing down in broad daylight they did and the terrible thing about them is they ain't got no pilot. There ain't a soul in these planes to fly the bloody things. You can see them overhead. We saw some but didn't know what they were, small planes, flames shooting out of the tail and the noise is deafening. But suddenly they go quiet 'cos the engine cuts out and they still go on flying for a while until the nose of the plane dips and then it comes speeding down to explode on anything that's in its path.'

Emily sat wide-eyed and shocked. 'Surely not more weapons!'

'You better believe it, my luv. Alf Woolston is a docker up in the East End but his mother lives just three doors up from me, and early this morning he came over to see if his old mum was all right. The tales he was telling us was enough t'make yer blood curdle. He said the damn things were exploding on hospitals, schools, factories, you name it, and all the ARP men said there was no defence against these planes.'

Emily shuddered. She was suddenly taken back to the night she had got caught up in London. Incendiary bombs had fallen on the city as if it were raining. It was the early hours of the next day before she was allowed into the underground car park in Whitehall and was given leave to drive her car out and make her way back to barracks as best she could.

Driving her car that morning, she would have best described it as a journey through hell. It was a journey that she would remember for the rest of her life. The whole sky had been glowing, lit up by the hundreds of fires that were raging across a city that had already suffered frequent violent assaults. She could still recall the awful smell of burning, of dust and smoke. At one point she had had to make a detour; the road was completely blocked and between the houses lay huge piles of wreckage. When she had realized that only a short while ago that wreckage had been family homes and that there was a possibility that people were still trapped beneath all that rubble, she had felt physically sick.

Emily sighed heavily, asking herself whether there was ever going to be an end to all this death and destruction.

Emily was washed and fully dressed. She had made the bed that Daisy and she had shared, and cleared up the breakfast things although she had been surprised at how much washing up there had been to do. It seemed that everyone must have set off in a terrific hurry to leave the place in such a muddle. She looked around the living room and her heart felt for Daisy.

Back up in Woolwich, their little house had been a palace. Now just look at this place! The very smell told you that no one had lived in this flat for ages. The paper on the walls was damp and peeling, the windows couldn't have been cleaned since the year dot. Daisy had had a go at them but they had dried pretty smeary. Yet she hadn't heard Daisy moan, not once.

Donald had had several digs. 'What had they come to now?' he repeatedly asked. She had great sympathy for Don, who was in his early fifties and still a good-looking man, though tending to heaviness about the middle. He was a typical Londoner, master in his own house – well, that's what the

Cockney women let their men believe because it made for a more peaceful life. He was feeling frustrated; he had always been the bread-winner but now he felt he wasn't pulling his weight. The dockyards and wharves were where he had always earned a living but the situation had got so bad that he never knew what to expect from day to day.

There was no more time for Emily to hark back over what had long gone, for Daisy had just come through the front door with Donald trailing behind her.

The big smile of welcome froze on Emily's face. They both looked so bad, she thought that there must have been a death in the family. She prayed one of their sons or daughters hadn't been in the area where these new planes that had no pilots had come down.

'Daisy, whatever is the matter? Just looking at the pair of you is frightening me. Come on, sit down and I'll make you a pot of tea.'

Daisy came and put her arms around Emily and held her tight for a full minute. Then she sighed. 'Oh dear, it's just one thing after another. I'm sorry we went off an' left you like that but we didn't 'ave much choice. By the way Tom said to remind yer that you've got a medical board tomorrow morning so he's going to come home as soon as his shift finishes an' take yer back down to Hythe.'

'Thanks, Daisy, I forgot that Tom had to work this morning. He couldn't have got much sleep.'

'Don't you worry that pretty 'ead of yours. Tom will be fine; he could sleep on a ruddy clothes line,' Donald told her, grinning but doing his best to reassure Emily. Then, almost as an afterthought, he called to Daisy, 'Didn't we see that café just across the common was open? Why don't we all go there and get ourselves a bit of breakfast? We didn't 'ave much earlier on an' it would save messing about 'ere.'

'Don, my old luv, you never 'ave a lot t'say but when you do you always come up trumps. That's a great idea.' Daisy was as pleased as Punch.

Then turning to Emily, Daisy asked, 'Would you mind if I were to ask Lucy from next door if she would like to come with us? She's been a right good neighbour, she 'as, in the short time we been 'ere, and she did step into the breach this morning. Once we're in the café I can tell yer all what's gone on this morning.'

Not before time, Emily thought, but she hadn't asked questions in case they thought she was too inquisitive.

'I think that would be a nice thing to do,' she said firmly.

Daisy got a bit of a surprise as she walked into the café. One of her old neighbours that she hadn't seen for a while was standing behind the counter.

'Well, I never! 'Ello, Dolly,' Daisy said, before she had hardly got a foot inside the door of the café, but sounding pleasantly surprised. 'It seems ages since we set eyes on each other – how come you're working 'ere?'

'Pretty much for the same reason you've come t'live in Manor Street. I heard you'd been bombed out. Settled in all right, 'ave yer, Daisy?'

'I wouldn't say that exactly, but like everyone else, it's a case of needs must when the devil drives.' Daisy sighed heavily. 'I didn't get much choice; don't suppose you did either. Lucky our landlord owned properties this side of the Thames but who's t'say we'll be any safer 'ere?'

'Don't think about tomorrow, that's what I tell myself. Anyway, four of you, is it, all wanting an 'ot meal?' Dolly asked, suddenly sounding all businesslike.

'That would be great,' Don piped up. 'It's good ter see you, Dolly luv. Can we 'ave four large teas t'be going on with?'

'Course yer can, me old mate, but we ain't got no sugar, only saccharine, an' to eat we got some streaky bacon, we got sausages but Gawd knows what's in 'em, and yer can 'ave fried egg but it's only dried egg. Yer don't get any yolk but yer can kid yerself it's an omelette.' Dolly had said all that as one mouthful, never once pausing to take a breath.

'That sounds great, but ain't yer going offer us no fried bread?' Don was trying to sound offended but he ended up laughing fit to bust.

''Ere, Donald Gaskin, make yerself useful and carry this tray over to where your good lady and 'er friends are sitting. I'll bring yer meals over as soon as they're ready.'

Don sat himself down facing Emily and the look of disbelief on her face told him that his dear wife had already told her that Tessa, their eldest daughter, was locked up in Holloway Prison.

''Ere, drink this,' he said, pushing a large thick mug full of steaming hot tea in front of Emily. Daisy and Lucy had already taken their mugs from the tray and were sitting, elbows resting on the table and hands clasped around the mugs.

'You haven't told me what charges the police are bringing against Tessa,' Emily reminded Daisy, who was staring vacantly across the café.

Don shook his head and took hold of his wife's hand before saying, 'Illegal off-course betting. In other words, unlawfully accepting bets, and being in possession of stolen goods.' He spoke as if he were reading the charges from a card.

'Tessa, that's Charlie's mother, isn't it?' Emily queried, frowning deeply.

'Yes, luv. You met her at our 'ouse. Charlie made a lasting impression on you, so Tom tells us. Tessa and Pete, that's 'er 'usband, 'ave two little girls, Patsy and Rosie, as well as Charlie, but there were so many in our 'ouse that day you came to see us that we couldn't expect you to remember them all.'

That had been a long speech for Donald.

'Are you sure that Tessa has been taken to prison?' Emily asked.

Don nodded his head. 'Yes, luv. This all 'appened two days ago, but no one thought to come an' tell us until this morning. Apparently the local remand home caught a blast and is out of action, that's why she's been remanded in custody at Holloway Prison. Seems they 'ad no option. The goods were found in Tessa's 'ouse and she was caught taking the bets.'

'Oh, no, she wasn't,' Daisy roughly cut in. 'She was trying to earn a few bob by letting the bookie's runner have a pitch in her doorway. Bert Pedlar his name is, and he'd just gone out the back to 'ave a pee when a punter came to the door wanting to place a bet, he 'anded a betting slip and four bob to our Tessa, she slipped it into her apron pocket and forgot it for the moment.'

'Yeah, well, bloody Bert got wind of the coppers being there, didn't he? He dropped his bag in Tessa's yard and made a run for it. He'll 'ave me t'answer to when I see him, believe you me,' Don said, sounding furious.

It was at that moment that Dolly came to the table carrying two hot plates. 'Get yer elbows off the table and get this down yer. Yer'll all feel better,' she said smiling, then added, 'I'll just fetch the other two.'

In spite of the shortages it wasn't a bad meal at all. Emily thought that the fried bread was particularly tasty and she said as much to Dolly.

Dolly didn't bother to tell her that a pig

farmer that came to the café to collect the swill had given her a great lump of pig's fat which she had rendered down to make a bowl of dripping and that was what the bread had been fried in.

Nobody spoke while the meal was eaten, except that Daisy did remark that they were the only customers and she wondered why.

'Cos you're in between times,' Dolly quickly put her straight. 'Six to nine we're busy with breakfast, tennish we do coffee and cakes when we've got any, half twelve till two is dinner time. All right?'

Daisy's mouth was full so she just nodded.

Emily was the only one who had left anything on her plate. The other three were as clean as a whistle.

Daisy took a deep breath, wondering whether she should put Emily in the full picture as to what had happened to their Tessa. She might be the sort of person who would be able to help, she being educated and all that. In any case she had told her most of it, there couldn't be any harm in telling her the rest.

'I can understand why my Tessa, and a good many more women, let a bookie's runner stand in their doorway. That's been 'appening for years and the few shillings they get paid would be worth a lot to them. Usually the magistrate turns a blind eye and lets the householder off with a small fine. Why? Because they like going to the races themselves an' if the truth be known they think it unfair that the man in the street can't have his small bet on the 'orses.'

Having heard all that, numerous questions flashed through Emily's mind and she felt sick with doubt, wanting to know how stolen goods came to be stacked up in Tessa's house yet dreading what the answer might be.

Suddenly Daisy decided she might just as well tell Emily the whole story. If she didn't she was sure that Tom would. It was a safe bet that he knew more about these goods than he was letting on.

'I'll start at the beginning, Emily luv, and tell yer what little I know,' Daisy said, wiping her hands on a big white handkerchief before starting. 'Going back some weeks ago, Tessa told me that she had been offered a job clearing out the contents of warehouses in London. Not big items, yer know; from what I've 'eard since, it's more like soft furnishings and all kinds of footwear, that had been soiled or damaged in the bombings. Fred Faulkner is the owner of the warehouses and he told Tessa that some goods had been too badly damaged for any stock to be salvaged.'

Gradually, the story took shape.

Where warehouses had been hit by a flash of incendiary bombs, the ARP men had used powerful water-jets on the fires that were raging throughout many buildings. In such cases it was water that had caused the most damage to the stock.

Mr Faulkner felt that a great deal of his stock could be saved. He needed sorters. Tessa and her mates needed the money. It was as simple as that. Fred Faulkner gave Tessa a free hand; she could employ three women to help her, but he wanted each place done thoroughly and he wanted it done quickly. All goods that could be retrieved were to be neatly stacked in crates that he was providing and all crates had been lined with clean linen. The number of goods damaged by dust and dirt, fire or water, were to be noted down on official forms that would enable Mr Faulkner to apply for the necessary compensation.

Then Don came back to the table with a packet of cigarettes and a box of matches. Emily wanted to ask how come some of the goods had ended up in Tessa's house, but instead she waited, hoping that Daisy would tell her without prompting just what had happened. But Daisy appeared to have forgotten; once again she was staring into space and it was Don who cleared his throat and spoke.

'According to our Tessa, half the time it was filthy work. Sheets and towels that were not only soaking wet but filthy dirty and stinking to high heaven, bedspreads and eiderdowns that had been scorched by the flames. Yet deep down in the packing cases a lot of the goods were all right, not a mark on them, but they did smell a bit of the smoke. It became a game with the girls. Damaged goods to the left and goods that could be retrieved put to the right.'

Don paused to drink his tea and to light a cigarette.

'In the beginning I think it started off in a small way. Each of the women were taking an odd pair of sheets or whatever it was that she needed most, an' who could blame them? All those things that you women set such great store by, yet 'aven't been able to lay yer 'ands on for years. Everything there could only be bought if you 'ad a docket from the Ministry of Supply and they're only dished out to young folk just getting wed or to those that've lost absolutely everything in a bombing raid.

'Then Alice Spencer had a brainwave, 'an before you ask how I know this,' he said looking directly at his wife, 'Alice herself told me, but she made a joke of it and I didn't think for one minute that she'd go ahead with such a scheme.'

'Well, whatever, you kept the whole bloody thing t'yerself, didn't yer?' Daisy angrily accused him.

'D'yer want me to go on or not?' Don's question was directed at Daisy but it was said very quietly.

Daisy didn't answer, she merely nodded her head.

Emily, Lucy, and even Dolly behind the counter, badly wanted to hear everything but of course it wasn't up to them. Silence reigned during which you could have heard a pin drop.

'You better 'ad,' Daisy said, suddenly sounding subdued.

'Well, Alice took to taking her six-month-old baby to work with her. Nobody gave a second look to a young mum pushing a pram. But then nobody knew that deep in the well of the pram, beneath where the baby lay, was a hoard of 'ousehold goods. Some needed a jolly good wash – so what? That didn't worry the girls.'

When Donald finally stopped talking, all the women in that Clapham café looked from one to the other. However, Daisy decided that they had washed enough of their own dirty linen in public so she quickly drained her teacup and stood up.

'Better settle up with Dolly and we'll be on our way,' she said to Don, before adding, 'Tom left home just after four this morning so he won't be too late getting home.'

Emily felt she had to be satisfied, but truth to tell she wasn't. She had been given a good idea as to where the goods came from, but how had the police made the discovery that a lot of them were in Tessa's house? And why, if there were four women involved, was Tessa the only one that was locked away in Holloway?

She knew she would have to curb her curiosity. She didn't have any option.

She'd have to wait until they got home to hopefully learn more.

# Seven

It was just after three o'clock in the afternoon when Tom walked in. He caught them all unawares, and the first thing he said was, 'What's the matter, has someone died?'

We must each of us be wearing that hangdog look, Emily decided, because that was the same question she had asked Daisy and Donald.

When no one bothered to answer him, Tom looked around at them with an impish grin. 'If it's Tessa you're all worried about, forget it – she'll be fine.'

'Oh, and you can guarantee that, can you, Tom?' Don said sarcastically.

Before Tom was given a chance to reply, Daisy was in there like a shot. 'What is it with you, Tom? You 'ear things almost before they ever 'appen. Have you got a direct line to something like a bloody bush telegraph system?'

Tom's grin spread from ear to ear. 'Something like that, Daisy. Just let's say bad news travels fast. Now just to make sure I've got the right end of the stick, Don, will you tell me exactly how many charges and what they are, that your Tessa is facing?'

Donald gnawed his bottom lip anxiously before saying, 'Look, lad, I know you'd do yer best for any member of this family but right now I've bin thinking it might be better to pay Tessa's fines and go an' bring her 'ome.'

Tom couldn't stop himself; he looked towards Emily and roared out laughing. It was a minute or two before he collected his wits and answered Don.

'Just like that, eh, Don? We walk up to the prison gates and tell them we got the cash an' we wanna buy our Tessa's freedom?'

Donald was so taken aback by Tom's cheek that he looked at him gobsmacked.

'Tom, you've never spoken t'me like that before so don't start now. I'd take a lot from you – you've been a good lad t'all of us – but that still doesn't give yer the right to take the piss out of me.'

Tom was immediately repentant. He hadn't meant it to sound the way it had come out. 'I am so sorry, Don, honestly I am. You didn't deserve that but it was the way you said it: "Let's pay her fine an' go an' fetch her 'ome." We don't even know if she will come up in front of a magistrate, and if she did maybe he would let 'er get away with a fine an' maybe he wouldn't; we'd 'ave t'wait an' see.'

Emily was appalled. 'Tom, are you saying there's a possibility that Tessa could go to prison?'

Tom gave a deep sigh. 'All of you, listen carefully to me, please. Yes, a magistrate would 'ave the power to sentence her to a period in prison and I can't guarantee that wouldn't 'appen if she did come up before one in court. Just the same, he could order that she pay a fine and be bound over for a period of say two years, but as it stands now we're only guessing. None of us know which way the case might go.'

Tom leant against the mantelpiece and gave them time for his words to sink in. Then very quietly he said, 'I don't think that anything of that kind is going to 'appen though.'

Daisy was up and out of her chair like a shot. Tears of relief were running down her cheeks as she threw her arms around Tom's neck.

'Oh, you're such a good young man. We was blessed the day you came to lodge in

66

our 'ouse.'

Tom untangled her arms from around his neck and held her away from him, but he was smiling broadly. 'Daisy, I am not a miracle worker but I do honestly believe we can get Tessa out from under this without too much 'assle.'

'Sorry I went for yer, Tom,' Don said, sheepishly.

Tom laughed. 'Made me realize what you're made of, mate. I admire you, always 'ave.'

Don held out his hand and Tom shook it. 'If there's anything that I can do, yer know you've only got t'ask,' Don said.

'As a matter of fact, Don, there's a couple of things you could do. First off, do you know if Tessa has actually been charged with anything?'

'Well, yes, Tom, the sergeant down at the station said she'd been charged with two counts, receiving and handling stolen goods, and illegally taking bets.'

'That's OK. Now, while I'm taking Emily back, could you put yer ear to the ground and find out which bookie was running Bert Pedlar and where he operates from?'

'No problem. I won't come back 'ere to-night until I've got everything you need to know. But there is one thing I'd like to ask you, Tom. Isn't the charge of stolen goods the worst of the two? Won't the court look badly on stolen stuff being in our Tessa's 'ouse?'

'They probably would if it were true.'

'But the coppers told Daisy an' me that they found it under the stairs.'

'Quite right, I expect they did. But I'm telling you that Jerry Faulkner is going to tell the truth. Those goods weren't stolen; he'd asked Tessa to do a bit of hand-washing and ironing. You get the picture?'

It took a minute for Don to smile, then he said, 'Gawd luv yer, son. Do you think he'll say that?'

'Oh, I *know* he will, Don. 'Ave no fears on that score, cos I've got a mate that knows a mate that is a good friend of Jerry Faulkner, and from time to time he's offered dodgy goods to a lot of people. Our Jerry is fond of boasting that it may be wartime but there is nothing that he can't lay his 'ands on and yer don't need coupons or dockets when yer dealing with him.' Tom stretched out his hand and smiling brightly he patted Don's shoulder. 'Now, he wouldn't want all that brought out in court, would he?'

The whole room was in an uproar. Even

68

Emily forgot that at most times she acted ladylike. She glanced across at Daisy and what she said had Tom nearly throwing a fit. 'Didn't know Tom was so well up in the criminal world, did you? Wait until I write my next letter to our parents. Should I tell them that our Tom not only deals in the black market but he makes a good advocate for someone who is in trouble with the law? Mainly because he, himself, has such a wide knowledge of the criminal world.'

As Emily finished speaking she winked at Daisy but Tom didn't see that.

'You wouldn't write such things to our mum and dad?'

'That depends,' she answered him cheekily.

'On what?' he asked, needing to know.

'On whether you stop at a decent pub on the way back to Hythe and buy me a decent drink.'

Tom didn't bother to answer her, but flung a cushion in her direction instead, missing her.

Emily had the last laugh; she threw it back and she didn't miss!

It was a lovely evening and Emily was thoroughly enjoying the drive. In fact it was so peaceful that she felt her head nodding and her eyelids closing.

Tom woke her from her slumber when he said, 'This is a lovely old-fashioned pub an' they have a garden out back. Shall we stop 'ere for a while?'

'Sounds good to me. Where are we?'

'In the small village of Rye,' Tom told her, as he steered the car on to the forecourt.

Emily got out of the car and shook her skirt to try to get the creases out. She was wondering whether or not she should change into her uniform when she got back to the convalescent home. She really did not want to be bothered tonight. She still felt tired and she would have to be up early in the morning and on parade in order to be taken before this medical board. Perhaps I can just slip in and get to my room without being seen, she thought hopefully.

'Em, what would you like to drink – is a G and T all right?' Tom's voice sounded aggressive, and another thing – he never shortened her name to Em. Sometimes other people did, but never Tom.

'Go through to the garden, find a table an' I'll bring our drinks out.'

Tom was ordering her to go and his face was like thunder as he walked away from her and went towards the bar.

Emily felt something was wrong, so she followed him. At the bar she touched his elbow and said, 'Tom, I don't want a gin. May I have something long and cool, please?'

'Such as?' It was said almost rudely; certainly his voice had a sharp ring to it.

'White wine and lemonade would be nice, Tom.' She spoke quietly, not wanting to make a scene in the bar, but once they were out in the garden she was going to ask why he had suddenly become so bad-tempered.

Tom didn't bother to answer but as Emily turned away she saw Captain Clive Beaumont coming towards her. Instinctively she stood still and drew herself to attention, then she caught Tom's eye, and realized that she didn't have to salute; she wasn't in uniform and she hadn't been on duty for weeks. About turn, and she was thankfully on her way to the outside garden. Let Tom deal with Clive since it was so obvious that he was put out by him being there.

She had quite a wait until Tom came out with their drinks. One look at him and she murmured, 'Thank the Lord for small mercies.'

'What made you say that?' Tom asked as he set the tray with their drinks down on the table.

'The very fact that you are smiling. From that fact alone I can tell that even if you did resort to a punch-up with his lordship, fisticuffs or verbal, it's obvious that you came out on top. Don't tell me that you sent him away with his tail between his legs.'

'Something like that,' Tom said, but he had the grace to look a bit shamefaced. 'He asked if I was taking you back to Hythe and I told him I was. Then he went all pompous on me when I refused his offer to take over from me. Tried hard to convince me that he would see you back quite safely.' Tom paused, chuckled to himself and picked up his pint and took a hefty swig.

Emily knew there was more to come and she didn't take her eyes off of Tom's face, but Tom was up to any game that she could play and it was Emily who at last showed her annoyance. 'There's got to be more to it than that,' she said harshly.

'Of course there was,' Tom placed his glass back down on to the table before saying, 'Clive had a lady with him. Apparently he had chosen to forget that fact as soon as he set eyes on you, but she must have tired of waiting and came to find him.'

'And?' Emily was practically spitting

feathers.

'Not much more to tell. The lady wrapped herself around Clive and told him he was a naughty boy for having left her waiting in the car for so long.'

Emily had just taken a sip from her drink but she almost choked because for the telling Tom had changed his voice, giving an impersonation of a highly-strung young lady who was very peeved.

'That was the end of our conversation. After that I didn't see his arse for dust.'

'Oh, Tom!' Emily was having a job to control her laughter. 'Are you telling me the truth?'

'Cut me throat if I'm telling a lie.' He grinned as he picked up his pint and took another good swig.

Emily took several sips of her own drink. 'This is delicious, thank you, Tom,' she said, smiling as she set her glass back down on the table. Then with a wicked glint in her eye, she said, 'I bet you never told him you were my brother!'

'I thought he knew.'

'I've never had cause to tell him.'

'Perhaps you should next time he offers to take you out.'

'What and spoil a very good friendship?'

Tom leaned back in his chair, and undid the top two buttons of his shirt. It had been a very long day but there was nothing that he wouldn't do for this lass that was sitting opposite to him. He admired her, loved the very bones of her, yet it was only affectionate love; to him she was just like a sister, part and parcel of his family.

Suddenly he said, 'Emily, shall I tell you something?'

'Would it stop you if I said no?'

'I'm being serious, sis. That Clive you've been knocking around with, he brings the worst out in me. I don't know why but he does; he really irritates me. He's so bloody sure of himself, looks down on everyone, yet you sometimes 'ang on to him like he was the brightest star in the sky.'

'How do you know how I act with him?' Emily was immediately up on her high horse.

'Because I've seen you up at the Rainbow Rooms, more than once. I haven't let you know I was there because I didn't want to spoil yer style. God knows you deserve a bit of pleasure. I think a whole lot of our youth has been snatched away from us because of this bloody war.'

When Emily didn't answer he added, 'No

74

one can blame any of us. Whenever the chance occurs, which isn't very often these days, we each of us plunge into a social life that would never 'ave been tolerated during peace time.'

'Tom, that was a big speech for you. You've been worrying about me, haven't you?'

'To be honest, Emily, yes, I have. Tell me, do you 'ave feelings for him? If not, what the hell d'yer see in him?'

'Well, first off he's a great dancer. I love being on the dance floor with him. I know I show off, but then so does he.'

'You mean he shows *you* off! Even in that stiff starchy uniform you always look good. You're slim with curves in all the right places, and every man in the room envies him.'

Emily had become very thoughtful.

Since meeting Clive she had been like a child in a lot of respects, pleased when he gave her presents, even though that wasn't very often. Looking back, she knew it had all been leading up to a weekend in Brighton. It hadn't even been a weekend – down on a Saturday afternoon, back in camp on Sunday evening. Why the hell had she agreed to go to Brighton with him? She was dead sure that his feelings for her didn't amount to much.

Suddenly, without giving the matter any thought, she found herself confessing everything to Tom.

'I went to Brighton with him, we stayed at an old-fashioned hotel. They served really good food, considering all the rationing.'

Tom laughed. Really laughed. 'Well, if that don't take the biscuit! You're telling me that the only detail of your time away with him you can remember was that the food was good. He certainly made a lasting impression on you.'

It was a great relief to her, hearing Tom laugh, but then what did she expect? He was very down to earth; she'd known that he wouldn't go off the deep end and he certainly wouldn't make a scene. He didn't tread the straight and narrow path himself, that much she did know.

Only one thought did scare her. When next Tom met up with Clive Beaumont, how would he react?

She had no way of telling.

Tom drained his glass, asked if she would like another drink, and when she said no suggested that they had better get on their way home.

Funnily enough, Emily was feeling tearful.

Would Tom think any the less of her because of her confession?

She looked up into his kind face and what she said made his heart ache.

'Oh, Tom, I wish someone would give me a break. I hate this war. I hate London. I miss my mum and dad and I miss Bella. And I miss John. I wish I could go home, go back to leading a normal life.'

'Don't we all, my darling, don't we all?' he murmured as he linked his arm through hers, and together they walked back to the car.

# Eight

Emma Pearson decided she would have a long chat with her good friend Agnes Brownlow on Saturday morning after they had both finished doing their shopping for the weekend. Emma had always found Aggie easy to talk to. She could not bring herself to discuss her problems with Sam, partly because he was too close. Aggie was more approachable and perhaps she could offer good advice.

Aggie shook her head sadly as they sat together in the market's little café as they did regularly every Saturday. 'Are you positive that the tablets that your Bella is taking really are just sleeping pills?' Aggie asked quietly. 'Myself, I always think there is a danger with sleeping pills. If they help in the short term they won't do Bella any harm, but she can't afford to become reliant on them. Besides, I think she's far too young to need sleeping pills.'

'That's what I'm worried about. To my mind Bella is overworked. Once she had settled that she was going to work on farms she really got into the life. Lately though, she's changed. As you know, Aggie, she was always such a bonnie lass; now there's no colour in her cheeks and she's always exhausted.'

'Do you think it *is* just a case of all work an' no play?' Aggie asked, looking very thoughtful.

'Quite the opposite, if I think about it. She's always going off somewhere and if it isn't with the Americans then it's the Canadians. I'm sure they're nice enough fellows but they're all that much older than Bella and they seem to be filling her head with such big ideas.'

'This war certainly has a great deal to answer for,' Agnes said, showing her concern, 'but if you don't feel right about the tablets, why don't you tell Bella that you are going to have a word with the doctor?'

'Oh, Aggie, you know I couldn't do that. Bella is an adult now, an' if I did go to the doctor he wouldn't tell me anything,' Emma said, managing to sound both wise and sad at the same time.

'I know where you're coming from, luv. We can see the mistakes our children are making and there isn't anything that we can do about it. Take my two boys – Lenny's eighteen soon and Sid will get his call up papers any day now. We can't keep tabs on them for ever and we certainly can't lead their lives for them.'

'This bloody war!' Emma exclaimed. 'The times I've heard people say, "Oh, it will all be over by Christmas!" Trouble is, they never say *which* Christmas. It seems to be going on for ever.'

'Have you heard from Emily lately? God knows she suffered a near miss, didn't she?'

'I like to think of it as a jolly lucky escape, but wait a minute...' Emma stopped talking and began to rummage around in her hand-bag. Pulling an envelope out, she held it up. 'Yes, I did bring it; thought I'd put it in my bag ... It's a letter from her, came a few days ago; here, I'll read it to you.'

*Dear Mum and Dad,*

*Being shunted into a crater by bomb blast has some compensation. I am now a fully-fledged non-commissioned officer, Corporal Pearson. Passed my medical OK.*

*Am being sent to Colchester, not allowed to give full address. Will be part of a driving pool, classed as light duties for a while.*

*Dad, this might put a smile on your face. We arrived safely at our destination. Big-wig, my passenger, had chosen to travel in the back of the car, he was working, papers strewn all over the back seat.*

*I got out of the car, brushed my uniform down with the flat of my hand, made sure the angle of my cap was correct. Then stood to attention making a very smart salute. FINALLY, the officer got out of the car.*

*'Very smart, Corporal,' he said, 'but in future try to remember to open the car door before you stand there saluting.'*

*Tell Bella she's lucky, she doesn't have to salute her bosses.*

*My love to Uncle John and Auntie Mary, and to Auntie Agnes, Len, Sid and Mary.*

*Tons of love to you two and to my dear sister. I miss all of you so much.*

*Emily xxxx*

As Agnes sipped her tea she thought about Emma's problem. It must be harder having two girls. Boys didn't seem to bring their problems home with them, a fact for which she was eternally grateful.

'How about Tom? Haven't seen so much of him just lately. Has he been in touch?'

Emma's face coloured slightly and she looked around quickly to see if anyone had heard. 'He spoke to Sam the other night. It's been a Godsend Ted Andrews giving Tom the telephone number of the pub and allowing Tom to ring there whenever he gets the chance. Almost every Wednesday evening about eight thirty he rings when he knows Sam will probably be in the bar, and if he's not Ted will always take a message.'

'Did he have much to say?' Aggie asked, curiosity getting the better of her.

Warning bells sounded in Emma's head. What had happened to Daisy and Donald's daughter wasn't something to brag about and she didn't feel it was right for her to sit here and discuss their family business.

'Mostly he was on about these doodlebugs, said he'd been up to Islington to visit a mate and while he was there one of these flying bombs had crashed down on to two blocks of flats. The whole lot was practically demolished, trees were uprooted, and residents that weren't killed had terrible injuries.'

'Good God,' Agnes said and breathed in heavily. 'We really don't know how fortunate we are, living tucked away down here.'

'Aggie, you never said a truer word. Tom was telling my Sam about Daisy. I've told you about her and her husband Donald and how welcome they made us on the couple of times we've been up to see them. Tom's always had good lodgings with them and since our Emily has been so poorly they've taken her under their wing as well. You knew they had to move 'cos their house was declared unsafe, didn't you?'

'Yes, that was a few weeks ago, wasn't it?'

'Yes, it was, but as it's turned out poor old Daisy is not her usual chirpy self. What with one thing and another everything seems to have got on top of her. In fact, I was thinking of asking my Sam whether he thought it would be a good idea if we brought her down to stay with us for a while. Give her a bit of a break like.'

'I reckon that would be the greatest kindness you could do for the poor woman, especially as you say she's made your Emily welcome.'

'Thanks, Aggie. 'Cos I'm not sure that she will want to come; she's got a big family all living somewhere near to her and Donald. I just wish I knew how Sam would feel about it. I don't want to put pressure on him. Perhaps I should stop turning it over and over in my mind and ask him outright.'

'Yes, you should,' Aggie agreed, doing her best to encourage her friend.

'Right, I'll bring the subject up tonight soon as we've had our dinner. Wonder what he'll have to say.'

'Knowing your Sam he'll be on the first train up to London.' Agnes paused and looked around the café. 'Only one thing you'd better watch out for,' she said, lowering the tone of her voice.

'Oh yeah, and what would that be?'

Agnes's eyes were twinkling with merriment as she said, 'That your Sam don't turn up here with a coachload. You said Daisy's got a big family and you know what these Londoners are like. They stick to one another through thick and thin. Ask one and you might just end up with the whole caboodle.'

Emma gave her friend a playful shove. 'Yes, and if I don't soon move from here, go home and get some dinner on the go, I may end up with no home for myself, never mind making the spare room up for Daisy.'

The look on Agnes's face changed as a group of American soldiers walked by just as she and Emma were coming out of the café.

'None of it makes sense, does it, Em?' she said, sighing heavily. 'There's those young men thousands of miles away from their families, and we're sending our soldiers, sailors and airmen, not to mention the merchant navy, to dangerous places around the world that half of them had never even heard of before this wretched war started. There's folk in every big city of this country losing their homes each and every day and if you listen to the wireless there is no end to the number of casualties.' She sighed again, before muttering, 'Where's it all going to end, Emma?'

'If I could answer that question, Aggie, the powers that be would have me up there in the city of London and I'd be treated better than the King and Queen are. But as I am not the brain of Britain we'd better get ourselves home.'

They walked along in silence for most of the way until they had reached the corner where Agnes turned off. Emma placed her shopping bags down beside her feet and took a moment's breather.

'By the way, Aggie, do you fancy a drink in the Fox tonight? We could pick you up about eight and you could walk up with Sam and me.'

'Yes, that would make a nice change. Thanks, Em.'

'All right, then, I'll be able to let you know what Sam has to say about me having Daisy come to stay for a bit of a holiday.'

Agnes laughed. 'He'll be all for it, you'll see. What he might have a hell of a lot to say about is if Ted hasn't had a delivery from the brewery! Your Sam doesn't go much on Alice's home-made wine.'

'Oh, did you have to bring that sour note into the conversation?' Emma asked, pulling a face. 'Just keep your fingers crossed, because if there's no beer Sam will be bringing us home early tonight.'

'I'll do better than that, I'll say a prayer,' Agnes said, grinning widely.

'And what makes you think that anyone up

there will listen to you?'

'Faith, my dear Emma, faith. Well, what little I've got left.'

'All right then, we'll see if it works. See you later.'

# Nine

Emma's mind was in a whirl. Without any hesitation whatsoever Sam had agreed that they should invite Daisy Gaskin to come and stay with them for a while, Donald as well if he could get away. It would do the pair of them good to have a break and they wondered why they hadn't thought about it before now.

Sam thought it best if he went up to Clapham; that way he would be in a better position to judge how things were for himself. That had been his way of thinking last night. This morning he'd been up at the crack of dawn and he'd changed his mind.

'Be much better if you come with me,' were the words he said as he shook Emma's shoulder and placed a cup of tea down on the bedside table.

Emma had raised herself up on her elbows and looked at the clock. It was only a quarter to six.

'What good would I be?' she'd protested loudly.

Sam wouldn't brook any argument. 'If Donald isn't able to come then it wouldn't be fair to ask Daisy to travel on her own with me.' That was his opinion and he didn't want any discussion. They had eaten breakfast in stony silence.

'Come on, Emma, be reasonable; you know it makes sense.' Sam got up out of his chair as he was speaking and Emma found herself being bundled out of the kitchen.

'But I'm not dressed and my hair needs washing,' she said as she was pushed along the hallway.

She went upstairs, still complaining. She didn't want to go to London, she didn't have the nerve for it. What if there should be an air raid while they were there?

An hour later she was sitting beside Sam in his van, which John Chapman, Aggie's brother, was driving, and they were on their way to Basingstoke railway station from where they would catch a train to Waterloo.

'Thanks for bringing us in, John. I didn't fancy leaving me van in the railway yard all day,' Sam said gratefully.

'Actually you did me a favour, Sam. I needed to come into Basingstoke to pick up supplies today and up at the farm petrol is non-existent at the moment. Are you counting on coming back this evening?'

Sam looked a bit uncomfortable. 'Emma thinks we are, and of course I'd like nothing better, but I'm not counting on it.'

'Give Ted Andrews a ring when you know what train you will be on, he'll get a message to me, and I'll be here to meet you.'

'Thanks, John, we'll see you,' Sam said and they shook hands as they parted.

The train journey wasn't going to be all that comfortable. Every carriage was pretty full and the corridors were wedged tight with soldiers and their equipment. They found one carriage which had no one standing, and as Sam slid the door open three women smiled, huddled up more tightly together and made room for Emma to sit down. Sam, being so tall, was able to steady himself by placing his hands on the luggage rack and so stand safely in front of his wife.

At the very next station three more people

squeezed themselves into the carriage and Sam looked down at Emma. 'Now you're getting a glimpse of how the other half live,' he said, with a smile.

Almost two hours later, when they came out of Waterloo Station, Emma stood stock still. What a difference to North Waltham! She was terrified of the noise, the pace at which everyone and everything moved; she wasn't used to anything like this.

Sensing how troubled Emma was, Sam gently took hold of her arm and led her back a few yards to where a café was situated inside the station.

'We'll see what they've got to offer,' he said as he pushed open the doors and saw that there were two or three vacant tables. He settled Emma down, made sure she was comfortable, and placed the bag he'd been carrying down at her feet. Then he raised his eyebrows in question. 'Do you fancy anything to eat?'

'Nothing to eat at the moment, Sam, but some nice coffee would go down well.'

Sam grinned. 'Coffee I may be able to purchase, but whether or not it will be nice is another matter.'

Then Emma smiled; it was the first time that she had done so since she had got out of her bed that morning. Sam had made a joke which told her that he was back to being good-natured. A sudden thought came to her; perhaps he hadn't wanted to travel to London on his own. He'd been more times than she had, though. At least twice he'd been here with the Reverend Michael Coyle when they had been searching for John and Tom. Dear Jesus, that seemed such a long time ago.

Sam stood at the counter waiting to be served. Two middle-aged women were unpacking sandwiches and cakes from deep-sided wooden trays, placing them into glass-fronted show cases. Sam felt he must be invisible because neither of them took a blind bit of notice of him; they were too busy telling their troubles to each other. They were both blondes, at least with the aid of a bottle of peroxide they were, and they must have plastered their make-up on with a trowel; that was the conclusion that Sam came to.

The smaller of the two women was close to tears as she stacked the sandwiches and placed a small flag on each pile showing details of what fillings were available.

'Peg, I don't fink I can stand much more,' she wailed.

The woman who had been addressed as Peg stabbed her cigarette out into a tin ashtray, and cleared her throat but still as she spoke her voice was husky from too many cigarettes and late nights.

'Aw give over, Rose; you should 'ave learned by now, they ain't worth it. We all find out in the end, I know I did. If I 'ad 'alf a dollar for every time I followed my old man, fought an' argued over him, I'd be a bloody sight richer than I am today.'

Sam had a job to cover his amusement.

At last Peg looked in his direction and putting on a cheeky grin she asked, 'What can I get yer, luv?'

'Do you have any coffee?' Sam asked in his most amiable voice.

'Yeah, we do as a matter of fact. Today yer can take yer choice, Camp bottled coffee or we've got some ground.'

'Ground coffee sounds great,' Sam said, smiling. 'May we have it made with half hot milk and half hot water, please?'

'Mister, now you're pushing yer luck.' Peg sounded serious, but she noticed that Sam was not trying to be clever, so she quickly said, 'Not from round 'ere, are yer, mate?'

'No, no, we're not. My wife and I have come up for the day to visit some friends.'

He nodded towards where Emma was sitting.

'Wherever you've come from, I wouldn't 'ang around too long if I were you. Yer obviously not used to shortages. Ain't many days when we get a delivery of fresh milk and when we do it don't go far. We got dried milk; it don't taste too bad, but then I'm used to it. It's better in coffee than it is in tea.'

'Thank you for telling me.' Sam felt foolish. 'May we have two coffees, please, and two of those jam doughnuts?' he said, pointing to an array of assorted cakes and buns.

'Course yer can, luv; go sit yerself down an' I'll bring 'em over t'yer.'

As Sam made his way back to sit with Emma, the door of the café opened and an air-raid warden came to sit at the table next to theirs. His face was ingrained with dirt, he had a cigarette in his hand and he drew deeply on it before saying, in a gruff smoke-filled voice that intermingled with his heavy coughing, 'It's bin a bloody 'ell of a night. Gets worse, don't it?'

Sam could only nod his head in sympathy and he was glad when Peg appeared with their order.

''Allo, gal,' the warden said, nodding toward Peg. 'Give us a large tea an' two of dripping toast, will yer?'

''Arry boy, you shall 'ave your toast in two shakes of a lamb's tail,' she told him.

Emma and Sam exchanged glances and both knew what the other was thinking: how in God's name did these Londoners keep so cheerful?

They sipped at their coffee and each got a pleasant surprise. It wasn't bad; in fact, it was quite good, Emma decided, as she took another few sips. The dried milk had given the coffee quite a creamy taste.

Emma felt that someone was watching her. She looked up and found that Peg was staring at her, and when she knew that Emma had cottoned on to her Peg raised her two thumbs in the air and grinned mischievously. Emma quickly returned the thumbs-up sign and then picked up her doughnut and bit into it.

Besides checking on how good the coffee was it was the effect of the doughnut that Peg had been waiting for. She was not disappointed. As Emma's teeth bit into the sugary concoction the bright red jam burst out, running down her chin.

Sam took notice, and being forewarned he

bit into his doughnut in a much more sedate manner. The customers had taken their cue from Peg and by now everyone in the shop was laughing. Not at Emma, but with her. Emma suddenly felt a whole lot more light-hearted. It must be true, what Tom was always saying: Londoners had a great sense of humour.

They finished their snack. Sam went to the counter to pay and when he slipped a six-pence into the staff box Peg leant across the counter and kissed his cheek.

Emma hesitated at the doorway and called out, 'Thank you, bye-bye.'

There wasn't one customer in the shop that refrained from calling out, 'Bye, luv, take care now, all the best.'

To Emma that chorus of voices had been an eye-opener. It was almost as if in the short space of time that it had taken them to drink their coffee and eat their doughnuts they had made a whole host of friends.

Once out of earshot, Sam said, 'It don't seem as if the Americans use that café.'

'How d'you work that one out?' Emma asked, sounding perplexed.

Sam chuckled. 'How many Yanks in our village wish you all the best, or tell you to take care?'

Emma took one look at his face and she too was giggling as she said, 'They prefer "Have a nice day".'

Sam was looking round trying to get his bearings. 'Now, if I remember rightly we have to cross Waterloo Bridge and get a bus to Clapham Common. So come on, Emma, best foot forward or it will be night-time before we arrive,' Sam said and he linked arms with his wife.

There were so many bus stops and even timetables, but no destination-boards, at the foot of Waterloo Bridge.

Well, they understood that. No place signs had been erased from North Waltham, maybe because the Borough Council had thought that the enemy would not be interested in such an out-of-the-way place, so small that they had never even been granted an air-raid siren, and they had never had to suffer the incredible ordeal of bombs raining down on their homes.

Sam decided that they should join a queue and ask the bus conductor to advise them of the best route to take to get them to where Daisy and Donald now lived.

All seats inside the bus were taken and folk were standing. There wasn't a conductor on board but a clippie, slim and neat in her grey dust-coat, her long fair hair tucked into a black lacy snood. With her leather money pouch slung over one shoulder and a wooden ticket-rack in one hand, she was cheerfully imploring the passengers to 'Pass along inside the bus, please.'

Sam and Emma hadn't got beyond the boarding platform when the clippie placed her arm across the couple who were in front of them. 'Sorry, my luvs, only twelve standing, but there's plenty of room on the top deck; climbing stairs is good for yer figure.'

'Well, she should know,' Sam said laughing, as they reached the top deck and found a double seat that was empty. 'She's as skinny as a greyhound.'

'I'm glad we've had to come upstairs,' Emma murmured as the bus pulled away from the stop. 'Just look at the view, we can see all over London.'

'So you're pleased I made you come with me now, are you?'

'So far I am, Sam, but let's wait until we've found where Daisy lives and get her back home safely with us, and then you'd better ask me again.'

'Playing the cautious card, are we?' Sam said, squeezing Emma's hand. He was thinking to himself that he didn't blame her for her fears. He'd be glad when they had done what they came to do and were on the train back home.

'Fares, please,' the chirpy clippie called as she passed along between the seats.

Sam already had some coppers and a half-crown in his hand, not knowing how far they were going to travel or how much the fare would be.

'Two to Clapham Common, please, or as near to it as you go,' Sam requested, smiling up at the young girl who was doing what would have been a man's job in peace time.

'Have you just landed from somewhere, mate? This bus goes to Golders Green and North Finchley, which are both in the opposite direction to where you wanna be.' Seeing that poor Sam looked flustered she brought her sympathy to the fore. 'I'll put you off at the next stop and then you've to cross the road and walk back to where you boarded this bus and you'll be almost out-side of Waterloo Underground Station. It's only five stops, Kennington, Oval, Stockwell, Clapham North and Clapham Common. The tube goes direct to Clapham, so you won't 'ave t'change at all.'

It was a bit of a palaver getting Emma

down the stairs while the bus was still moving and she was thankful when she was standing safely on the pavement.

Sam thanked the young lady and stood on the edge of the kerb watching as the clippie rang the bell and her bus moved off.

He had helped Emma down the stairs of the bus but it was only now, as he took her arm in readiness to cross the road, that he actually looked at his wife. Her face was as white as a ghost. She was trembling. She couldn't, or at least she wouldn't, move.

Sam stood facing her and took hold of both of her hands. 'Goodness me, whatever is the matter, Emma? Don't you feel well?'

'I feel all right, but I am not going to go down and get on that London underground train.' Emma's voice was flat but her words left him in no doubt that she meant what she said.

'Whatever has got into you?' Sam asked sharply.

'You know very well what Tom has always told us about the tube stations and how whole families practically live down there on the platforms.'

'So, doesn't that tell you that they must be one of the safest places to be if and when an air-raid siren is heard?' Sam was doing his best to sound convincing and at the same time doing his best to be patient.

'What about the tube stations that have received a direct hit and everybody down there has been killed?'

Poor Emma, she sounded so vulnerable and now was not the time or the place to stand and argue. Very firmly Sam took hold of her arm, and as soon as there was a break in the traffic he practically marched her across the road.

'We are going to the tube station and before you say a word there will possibly be a taxi-rank there – that's if the drivers have got any petrol. If there is, then I will hire a cab, which will hopefully take us right to Daisy's front door. Will that suit you?'

He was rewarded by seeing Emma visibly let out a sigh of relief.

They were lucky; a cabbie was just driving on to the forecourt as they arrived. Letting go of Emma's arm, he said, 'Stay here, don't move. I'm just going to have a word with the cab driver.'

Emma leaned against the wall, still struggling to stay calm, wishing with all her heart that she had never allowed Sam to talk her into coming with him to this noisy, dirty, busy city, forgetting for the moment that it had been her idea in the first place to bring Daisy away from all this hustle and bustle. Barrow boys were shouting their wares, and newspaper-vendors were yelling, 'Read all about it.' It only needed a siren to go off and she would really go to pieces. Why was so much noise necessary? Did nothing happen up here in a quiet orderly fashion? At home in North Waltham, even at their open-air market on a Saturday, the noise was never anywhere near as bad as this. No wonder Daisy wasn't coping so well.

The taxi driver was a big man and a true Londoner. Having been told of the reason they were in London and where they wanted to go, also that Emma wasn't feeling so good, he was out of his cab in no time and walking beside Sam to where Emma was still leaning against the wall.

The cabbie held out a huge hand. ''Ello, luv. I'm Butch.'

Emma didn't even raise her head.

'Come on, me old darlin',' he said, taking in the situation at a glance. 'Yer first time up in the smoke, is it?'

Emma stared at him with slight suspicion then, in a soft voice, said, 'No, I have been before, but never since the war started. I'm sorry, I can't help it, I'm scared stiff.'

'Well, luv, first fings first. Let's get yer coat orf, yer look as if yer sweltering. Then we'll get yer in me cab an' we'll be orf.'

Emma was wearing what she still regarded as her new coat even though Sam had bought it for her a couple of years ago. It was double-breasted and quite smart with a velvet collar, but the material was a heavy tweed. Sam undid the buttons and he stood one side of her and the cabbie the other while they helped her off with it.

Funny, was her immediate thought, but she did feel better already. The dress she was wearing she had made herself and she was proud of it. Navy blue with white collar and cuffs, she felt it was smart.

Sam carried her coat and Emma managed to smile as the cabbie offered her his arm. After only a moment's hesitation she linked her arm through his and within a few minutes she and Sam were seated side by side in the back of his London taxi.

The cabbie kept up a running commentary about the areas they were passing through and Sam was genuinely interested. Butch told him how London's famous landmarks, St Paul's Cathedral, the Houses of Parliament and Buckingham Palace had all been damaged.

The jungle of London's back streets showed all the signs of being war-torn. There were bombsites galore, and where once there had been panes of glass to let the daylight into homes, now there was always darkness because windows shattered by bombblasts hadn't been replaced, merely boarded over.

For Emma the journey didn't do much to settle her fears.

As the cab took them through South London the region did seem a bit cleaner, even more green, she decided, as she looked at trees and hedges, and to a certain extent they were leaving behind a lot of the debris which the bombing of London had caused.

Half an hour later the cab came to a halt outside Number 4, Manor Street. Manor Street was wide, comprised of two rows of tall terraced houses divided halfway down by Navy Street.

'You feeling better now, missus?' Butch asked as he helped Emma out of the taxi.

'Yes, yes I am, and I do thank you for your kindness.'

'Say no more,' Butch said, grinning. 'You 'ave a nice time with yer friends.'

Sam stood beside Emma and watched as Butch turned his cab around and drove off.

'A little help is worth a deal of sympathy, isn't it, Emma?'

'It certainly is, Sam. We've been lucky so far – everyone we've met has gone out of their way to be kind.'

They both now turned to look at the property where Daisy and Donald were living. 'I know from the address that Tom gave us that it is a basement flat but how the devil we find the entrance I just don't know,' Sam said, almost as if he were talking to himself.

They moved closer to the main entrance of the house and saw that in the small front garden an elderly man was perched on the window-sill and an elderly woman was sitting on a low chair, her knees covered by a huge patch-worked quilt. The man had a flat black cap on his head and the woman was wearing a straw bonnet.

'Sorry to trouble you,' Sam said, 'but I wonder if you can tell me where the entrance to the basement flat of this house is?'

'Course I can, mate, turn around and walk back a few steps. Look over the low wall an' you'll see a flight of steps that lead to their front door. Daft way to 'ave t'obtain entry if yer ask me.'

At that instant Daisy's head appeared over

the top of the wall as if on cue.

'Well, I'll be blowed, I don't believe it! I'm utterly flabbergasted, not that I ain't thrilled to see yer both ... but how the 'ell did yer get here?' Daisy sounded as stunned as she looked.

'Good afternoon, Daisy,' Sam said quietly. 'More to the point, how do we get into your flat, or do we have to spend the rest of the day standing here on the pavement?'

'Oh my Lord, I'm sorry.' Daisy's head disappeared and in two ticks she was up the steps and had her arms around Emma. Turning her head to look at Sam but not releasing her hold on Emma, she said, 'Follow me, and mind 'ow yer go, the steps ain't exactly in good condition.'

They followed her through her open front door, down a short narrow passage way and into a surprisingly cheerful-looking living room. 'Oh, dear,' Daisy sighed.

'Why the heavy sigh, Daisy?' Sam asked with a note of exasperation in his voice.

''Cos in less than an hour I got to go to the prison. I'm 'oping an praying that I'm gonna bring my Tessa 'ome with me. I'd better make yer a cuppa before I go.' Daisy sighed again, shaking her head slowly.

It was as if Emma came to life, because she

immediately took charge.

'Daisy, you sit yourself down and tell Sam all that has happened since he spoke on the telephone to Tom. We don't need a cup of tea just yet. Sam and I had a coffee at the station when we got off the train.'

Daisy seemed relieved, as she settled herself in an armchair and started to talk to Sam.

Emma walked to the second window that was on the opposite wall of the room, and found that she was smiling. Outside there was a garden, so she supposed the flat had to be on two levels. From the street you came down a flight of stairs, but instead of the flat being a dungeon, once down there it was on the level of what could be a fine garden. It was a really nice size, and Emma found herself thinking of all the things that could be grown out there if only someone would take the trouble to clear away all the rubbish and turn the earth over.

'Emma, I think you should come and listen to what Daisy has to say,' Sam called to her, sounding rather forceful.

Emma was brought back to today's happenings with a sharp jolt. She wasn't sure she wanted to hear whatever it was about. Time was getting on, it was already early afternoon, and the thought of them being able to persuade Daisy to get on a train with them, and that they might all be home to sleep safely in North Waltham by nightfall, was a wish that was fast fading.

# Ten

Daisy gave Emma a friendly smile.

'I'm so sorry I ain't given either of yer much of a welcome, but I really don't know whether I'm coming or going today. Our Tessa 'ad to appear in the South Lambeth Magistrates' Court this morning. Her father was gonna be there but when it turned out that he wasn't gonna be able t'make it Tom said he'd go, say he was a relation like; much better if a bloke stands up for yer, so they say. I couldn't do it as I'd go ter pieces for sure.'

Sam felt that Daisy was wandering from the subject but then again if it were Tom that had appeared in court on Tessa's behalf they wouldn't get to know the facts until Tom himself put in an appearance.

'How is Donald?' Sam asked, quickly changing the subject.

'Oh, I don't suppose you've 'eard,' Daisy said, all solemn. 'He slipped when he was down in the hold of one of the ships – 'ad an awful job getting him up, they did – and 'e's bin off for a fortnight now with a bad back. These last three days I've 'ad him up, got him sitting in a chair. The union doctor's bin once, said 'e should apply fer a lighter job 'cos his back ain't never gonna 'eal properly. What d'yer think about that? I asked the doctor if he was joking, and when he said he wasn't I asked him, 'ow the bloody 'ell can a docker apply fer a light job? Didn't get no answer, did I?'

Daisy paused and took a couple of deep breaths.

'Anyway he's taking to going to the pub again so he can't be in that much pain,' she added, pretty much as an afterthought.

It was Sam who sighed with relief as he heard footsteps coming down the steps and Tom's voice calling, 'It's only me.'

To say Tom walked in would not be true – he breezed in. 'Hi, Daisy, get the kettle on, I'm dying for a cuppa. Hallo, Aunt Em, I never thought to see you 'ere in London, not in wartime I didn't.' He wrapped her in his arms and, without releasing her, he looked up at Sam. 'Great work, Sam, getting Aunt Em to leave her beloved village. I'll 'ave a quick wash and then you can tell me what it is that has brought you to this dangerous part of the world.'

'Hey you, young man, wait a moment,' Sam begged him. 'You don't sound a bit surprised to see us. How did you know we were here?'

Without giving Tom a chance to answer, Daisy was straight in. 'It would be Lucy Bannister from next door. Ten ter one she saw you arrive and I'll bet there ain't much of our conversation that she's missed out on either. Walls 'ere are paper-thin and I bet she was watching out for Tom, but there again she always is. Fancies our Tom, she does, no getting away from that fact.'

'Daisy, my darling,' Tom said, grinning from ear to ear, 'you reckon our neighbour fancies me – well, so does every female I work with. And when I'm walking the streets I 'ave to brush the women aside. I can't 'elp it if I'm irresistible.'

Both Emma and Sam had to hide their smiles behind their hands. Tom had got one thing right. He was irresistible! It was as they had always known, everybody loved Tom; cheeky beggar he was, but nonetheless he got by.

Tom came back in from the scullery, stripped to the waist, drying himself on a rough bath towel. 'Will somebody please make the tea? And then I don't know about you lot but I'm going to chance me arm and pay Holloway Prison a visit.'

Daisy was already in the scullery setting out cups and saucers on a tray while she waited for the kettle to boil. She popped her head around the doorway and called, 'I was going to go myself 'cos Don said they had to let me see Tessa as she is only on remand, but I don't know if that's right or not though.'

'We can all go if you like. I've got a motor outside, and I'll tell you what happened in court as we go.' Tom made the offer, but only half-heartedly.

'You were in court?' Daisy queried, sounding astonished.

'Yes. Don met me when my shift finished last night, that's why I was up and out before you were about this morning.'

'So, what 'appened?' Daisy was getting really impatient.

'I'm going into me bedroom to get

changed, then I would like a cup of tea and to get going.' Looking towards Sam he asked, 'You and Aunt Em coming? It's not a bad ride and I'll take you for a meal after.'

Sam would have preferred to have some time with Tom on his own, to explain why he and Emma were here and to ask a few questions of his own. Now was not a good time, he decided. Like his wife, his hopes of being on the train back to North Waltham today were fading fast, but he was going to give it a damn good try. They had only been here for half a day and already he felt sure they had both had more than enough of London.

When everyone had been given a cup of tea, Daisy bustled about getting herself ready. She had already dressed herself in the only smart costume that she possessed but hadn't worn for ages, its straight brown skirt falling about two inches below her knees, and the well-fitting jacket nipped in at the waist. She had been relieved when she had tried it on this morning and found that she could still get into it and do up the four buttons. Beneath the jacket she was wearing a fawn-coloured silky blouse that didn't have a collar, just long double lengths of material at the neck, which she had tied into a floaty-looking bow which was quite attractive. Her hair fell naturally into waves and she held it in place with a side comb placed behind each ear. Daisy wasn't very tall and she was inclined to be a bit dumpy, but as she forced her feet into a pair of plain brown high-heeled court shoes there was quite a trans-formation.

'I just 'ope we don't 'ave t'walk miles 'cos these shoes are killing me already,' she moaned as she gathered up the cups and saucers and took them through to the scullery.

'Daisy, for God's sake will you stop doing that and come and get in the car?' Tom pleaded.

It seemed as if half of Manor Street was standing watching as the four of them came up the steps to get into the car.

Sam sat up front with Tom while Emma and Daisy were comfortable in the back.

'It's at times like this that I wish we'd never had to leave Woolwich,' Daisy loudly declared. 'In our old street folk would 'ave come over to us, to wish us and our Tessa all the best, but this lot in Manor Street ain't said a word.'

'Aw now, Daisy, be fair,' Tom called over his shoulder. 'We ain't lived 'ere five min-utes, so they don't know us any more than we know them. Lucy next door is all right now you've got to know her, isn't she?'

'I suppose,' Daisy half-heartedly agreed, thinking it better if she kept her mouth shut for a while.

When asking if Emma and Sam would like to come along for the ride, Tom had told them it wouldn't be a bad journey. Emma had taken that to mean that the country-side might be nice. How wrong she was. Clapham was in South London, and Hollo-way Prison was in the borough of Islington in North London. The journey wasn't at all pleasant, at least not to Emma. The visible signs that London had taken a terrific pounding from the Germans were every-where she looked.

As Tom drove down Holloway Road Emma perked up.

Highbury Corner the street sign said. Never in the whole of her life had she set eyes on such wonderful buildings or ever would again she was thinking. There was Highbury railway station, and the Cock Tavern, and to the right a number of large private houses the like of which she had never known existed.

Holloway Road ran through the centre of the town and soon Tom was pulling up outside the prison. It was certainly a grim-looking building, yet when Emma closed her eyes she was able to tell herself that she could visualize this place having originally being built as a castle, mainly because it had so many towers and turrets, and she thought its external walls must be excessively thick. There were giant iron railings to the front with tall gas-lit lamp posts on either side of the huge main gates.

Daisy was out of the car almost before the wheels had stopped turning. Tom was forced to put a restraining hand on her arm and say, 'Now, Daisy, promise me you'll take it easy, no shouting yer mouth off. You and I might be allowed to see Tessa because she is still on remand, but I am not a hundred per cent sure that she'll be released this afternoon.'

In actual fact Tom knew darn well that Tessa was going to have to remain in custody because the main witness for Tessa's defence had not bothered to show up this morning. But he wasn't going to let on about that to Daisy, not until she was in a place where she would have to control her temper.

As for Jerry Faulkner! Tom's blood was boiling. He personally was going to make sure that Faulkner would live to regret having made such a bad decision. He had always understood that Jerry was astute when it came to business. Craft and cunning was to be expected from his sort, but not this!

He'd got Tessa to round up three of her mates and had set all of them working in his warehouses where a great deal of his stock had been spoiled by fire, water and general bomb damage. 'All above board' is what he had promised those girls.

But when was Mr Faulkner's business all above board? His claims for compensation would be grossly exaggerated, that went without saying, and nobody would be blaming him for that. God helps those who help themselves.

Tessa and her mates knew the score, so who the hell was going to blame them if they helped themselves to a little of what was going? God alone knows, those young women had put up with all the shortages for four years now, and let's face it, only saints would have worked in those warehouses and not helped themselves to a few household goods and a couple of pairs of shoes for their kids.

Tom leant against the car waiting for Daisy and Emma who had gone off to spend a penny. He shook his head. He'd sent word to Faulkner making it known that if he knew what was good for him he'd make sure that no charge of theft was brought against Tessa Kennedy, and he'd also put Pete, Tessa's husband and the father of their two little girls, in the picture.

Pete Kennedy was a big man, and an Irishman to boot, and he was not known for his quiet temperament. If Faulkner wanted a private war on his hands he was going the right way about it. Tom knew that all he had to do was wait.

He'd go into the prison with Daisy and see Tessa, assure her this was only a minor setback and that she would be released very soon. That the officer in charge would allow them a short visit Tom had no doubt; a few folded fivers could easily be slipped into the gentleman's hand.

He was wondering where Sam had got to when he saw him shepherding his wife and Daisy back across the main street. That put an end to his ramblings; he pulled his shoulders back sharply and told himself that the quicker he got this visit over the better. However, his mind still lingered on Jerry Faulkner. Life would have been so much easier if that slimy bloke had turned up this morning, and told the magistrate that the goods found in Tessa's house were there with his permission and that they had not been stolen.

Mr Faulkner was going to regret the fact that he hadn't.

Tessa had already spent three days in custody on remand and once she was free it was going to take a lot to pacify her! And her husband.

'God give me strength,' poor Daisy murmured, when Tom asked if she was ready to go. Emma felt so sad and so sorry for her, wondering how she would feel if it were one of her daughters locked up in prison.

'You two don't mind waiting in the car, do you? I don't think they would let four of us in.' Tom was speaking directly to Sam, but it was Emma that quickly answered, 'I don't think I could bring myself to enter that place even if they paid me.'

'All right, then, have a walk about, stretch yer legs if you want, but don't go far away from the car.' Tom laughed as he added, 'It don't belong to me so I don't want to come out and find it 'as bin nicked.'

Sam and Emma looked at each other and they both chuckled as Tom took Daisy's arm and together they walked through the gates.

'He doesn't alter, does he?' Sam said.

Emma replied, 'We wouldn't want him to.

He's growing into a fine young man.'

They both decided not to sit in the car. Finding the gates to Holloway Prison were wide open they even dared to walk some way along the wide path. On each side stood some magnificent tall trees. Emma was thinking to herself that these front grounds were beautiful and very well kept, when suddenly she heard Sam utter loudly, 'Well, I never!'

There was such amazement to be heard in his voice that Emma stood still and remained quiet until he called, 'Emma, come here and read the inscription on this foundation stone.'

Sam reached for Emma's hand and held it tightly as they stood side by side and read: MAY GOD PRESERVE THE CITY OF LONDON AND MAKE THIS PLACE A TERROR TO EVIL DOERS.

'Makes you shudder, doesn't it?' Emma said, her voice scarcely above a whisper.

'It most certainly does,' Sam agreed. Then looking down at his wife, he said, 'You know, Emma, we haven't spoken a word to Daisy about the reason we came to London today and she hasn't passed any remarks either – well, not really. She did show surprise when we first arrived, but since then she has just accepted that we are here.'

'My thoughts exactly,' Emma replied. 'Do you think we could get away without asking her if she wants to come home with us?'

Sam had the grace to look guilty. 'I was beginning to wish something like that. I don't know about you, Em, but I don't think for one moment Daisy would feel at home in North Waltham. She leads such a different life up here, don't you think?'

'Yes, I agree. All the same, what I just said about not asking her was most uncharitable, so I think we should put the offer to her, see what she has to say. Poor woman, she really does look all in. If she doesn't get a break I fear she is going to be really ill. Though what she will do all day if she does come to us for a holiday I dread to think. She could come to the Women's Institute, and she could do a bit of gardening, but I don't think either of those options would be to her liking. And another thing—' Emma stopped short.

Sam prompted her, 'Finish what you were going to say.'

'Well, it's her smoking, I watched her out in the scullery, and even just now, when we were in the toilets, she lit one cigarette from another. Goodness only knows how many packets she gets through in a day.'

'Or where she gets them from,' Sam said with a laugh. 'Seems to be the general habit; almost everyone we've come into contact with has been a heavy smoker. Can't blame them, not with all the strain that they've been living under.'

Inside Holloway Prison things weren't exactly working out as Tom had planned. The Prison Officer had palmed the folded notes from Tom's hand to his own and then into his trouser pocket without so much as a blink of his eyes.

Turning to Daisy, he said, 'I'll have your daughter brought along to the visiting room, Mrs Gaskin; it's not in use at the moment and I can give you ten minutes.' He had spoken kindly, having noted Daisy's surname from the visiting form he had just asked her to sign.

Tom held his breath, waiting for Daisy to lose her temper and swear at him. Ten minutes wouldn't be what she'd had in mind.

The room they were shown into was cold and pretty bare, the walls painted green, with cheap rickety tables and chairs laid out in straight rows. There was a high platform at one end of the room, which was where the prison warders would normally stand and oversee the prisoners and their visitors, or so Daisy had already presumed.

'Mum, listen to me,' Tessa pleaded; their hands were linked tightly. 'I don't want you laying awake at night worrying yerself sick over me. The magistrate couldn't 'ave been more on my side if he'd tried. From what I gathered he likes a flutter on the gee-gees himself, though course he never said so. He asked me 'ow come I'd let a bookie's runner use my doorstep to take bets. I told him straight, I'd been sweet-talked into it and lured by the few shillings a week he was paying me; after all, where was the 'arm in it. I wasn't 'urting no one.'

'Oh, Tessa luv, it's not right you being 'ere,' Daisy moaned. 'You've done nothing wrong.'

Tom thought it was time he took over. 'Tessa, you know what you were told: the magistrate couldn't give a verdict because you were facing two charges. On the one of you accepting illegal betting slips, he as good as said he was going to let you off with a fine, though nothing definite, mind. On the other charge you pleaded not guilty and the solicitor said your employer was going to give evidence.'

'Yeah, yeah, I was there, remember, so I

know all about it. But what that bugger Faulkner is supposed to 'ave said an' what he did are two very different things.'

For all her bravado Tessa was very close to tears. Tom was on his feet straight away and took her in his arms.

'Oh, Tom, what am I going to do? I've tried so 'ard t'keep me pecker up but the crying and screaming at night is driving me mad. It's so cold and dark in those cells.'

She sniffed and pulled a handkerchief from the pocket of the dark blue cotton dress she had been given to wear, and when she had given her nose a jolly good blow she looked at her mum and asked, 'Why isn't my Pete with you? An' what about me dad?'

Daisy rubbed at her eyes and sat up straight.

'Yer dad's going barmy. He would have come with us but he's gone to see Ron Leadbetter – he's the bookie who was paying Bert Pedlar to collect the bets from your 'ouse. Yer dad will make sure he sees you all right and he'll make certain Mr Leadbetter pays any fine they throw at yer.'

'Thank Dad for me, Mum, but you still ain't told me why Pete 'asn't come?'

'I can tell you that.' Tom thought it about time he broke this up before they were told their time was up. 'I went to see Pete late last night. There's still a few of your good neighbours left in Woolwich, ain't there?'

'Only 'cos our street is three streets away from where those bombs fell. We got most of our windows blown out but otherwise we were pretty lucky. At least we ain't been turfed out of our 'ome.'

'Yeah, well, when Pete got home from work last night he went to yer neighbours to pick up your two girls and apparently they were in a right old state. Rosie was the worst, seemed to think yer wasn't never coming home again. Pete got on to his boss who told him to take some time off, to stay and see to the girls himself.'

By now Tessa was in floods of tears and there was nothing they could do for her. Two officers were holding the door wide open and nodding their heads, indicating it was time for them to leave.

Hard to tell who was suffering the most, mother or daughter. Tom put his arm around Daisy's shoulders and led her away, doing his utmost to prevent her looking back.

Tessa's crying echoed in their ears all the way down the long walk to the main gate.

As the warder watched them walk away his

main thought was that Tessa Kennedy should never have been in here. Probably she wouldn't have been if she'd spoken up for herself instead of being such a secretive bugger. Never a word in her own defence in case she dropped her mates in the shit. In this life you could carry friendship too far, at least that's how he looked at it. His every instinct told him that when she was released she was going home to a load of trouble.

He was dead right.

# Eleven

Daisy sat curled up in the corner of the back seat of the car, crying quietly. Emma's heart ached for her, so she leaned across and patted her shoulder.

'Daisy, sit up and wipe your eyes, please. I want to talk to you.'

'What can you possibly 'ave t'say that will be of any 'elp?' Daisy said ungraciously, wiping her eyes with a handkerchief that was already sopping wet.

'You are quite right, nothing that I can think of to say will help your Tess. But Sam and I have a proposition to put to you that might just do you a power of good.'

'Oh, yeah? I don't see 'ow anything is going t'be good for me, not at the moment I can't.'

'Well, the reason that Sam and I came up to London today was to ask you if you would like to come back with us, have a holiday, a short break away from all the stress and what-have-you that you've had to put up with. How do you feel about it?'

'Feel about it? If I didn't know you for the good woman you are, I'd say you was 'aving a laugh at my expense.'

'Oh, Daisy,' Emma was quick to cry. 'The offer was never meant to be a joke, truly it wasn't. We felt we would like to even things up a bit. There's you and your family suffering the air raids night after night, and where we live – well, sometimes we tell ourselves that the war hasn't affected our village, though of course you know very well that we lost John soon after the outbreak of the war.'

Daisy was immediately conscience-stricken; she grabbed one of Emma's hands and held it between both of hers. 'I'm sorry, luv. God knows losing John left its mark on Tom, though he acts all brave most of the time. As for you and Sam – well, as I said at the time, it was a rough deal and I am sorry.'

The silence hung heavy until Sam half turned around in the front passenger seat, put his arm through the front seats and patted Daisy's knee. 'Truly, Daisy, the only reason we made the journey today was to ask you to come home with us. We hear from Tom of all that you've had to put up with, and we feel helpless half the time, so we thought you deserved a break.'

'God love yer, both of yer,' Daisy said, her tears now changing to a slow smile. 'But tell me, what on earth would I be doing stuck down in the country miles away from anywhere and only cows and sheep to talk to, according t'what Tom tells me?'

'It isn't half as bad as Tom seems to have made out,' Emma said, sounding as if her feathers had been ruffled.

'Oh, no, please don't get me wrong. I was deliberately exaggerating. I'm sure it's not like that at all. But I couldn't leave me family; I'd miss them and by Gawd they'd miss me. If I'm not needed for baby-minding, it's Mum, will yer meet the kids from school; Mum, will yer queue up at the fishmongers cos he's had some 'addock come in; Mum, will yer take me bag-wash in when they drop it on the doorstep; Mum, if yer can spare the time my ironing ain't half piling up. Oh, yes you can all laugh yer 'eads off but I do 'ave me uses. And that's another thing – Sundays, some of me kids come to breakfast even if all I've got t'give them is beans on toast, then no sooner do we get rid of that lot an' Don an' me 'ave washed the dishes than the second lot arrive. Mind you, they always bring something with them and Tom 'ardly ever fails to get us a bit of meat from somewhere. Then there's Sunday tea, with more kids than we know what t'do with and some of 'em don't even belong t'the family – me boys say they bring them along to give their mothers a rest. Never mind about this poor old mother!'

At last Daisy stopped talking.

Emma was clutching her sides, which ached from the amount of laughing she'd done. Sam was wiping his eyes and Tom had had a job to keep his eyes on the road.

'So I take it that you don't want to accept our hospitality?' Sam said, having the greatest difficulty to keep a straight face.

'Yer don't really mind if I don't come an' stay with yer, do you?' Then, having given way to a hearty chuckle, Daisy added, 'Honestly, can you see me watering yer flowerbeds and digging spuds? I'd be a raving lunatic inside of two or three days. Anyhow, Tom reckons he's going to buy his own car as soon as this bloody war is over, then he'll be able to bring me down t'see you for the day. By the way, yer welcome t'stay the night at our place, though Gawd knows where we'll all sleep. Are you 'ome tonight, Tom?'

Again Sam, Tom and Emma were laughing fit to bust. It was as if somebody or something had wound Daisy up, because once she started talking she never seemed to stop to take a breath.

Almost on cue she leaned forward and said to Tom, 'Have you any idea where we might find Don?'

'You told Tessa her father had gone to see Ron Leadbetter, an' if that's right I know exactly where he'll be – in the pub down by the docks.'

'Can we pick him up? Or is it out of yer way?'

Tom didn't answer but he slowed the car down and as soon as he saw a space by the kerb he drove the car alongside, parked it and switched the engine off.

'Now let's get things sorted out. Sam, are you aiming to go home tonight?'

Sam and Emma answered in unison, 'Yes, please.' They both laughed.

Sam said, 'Tom, have you any idea what time the last train to Basingstoke leaves Waterloo?'

'Course I 'ave. Been on it a few times, 'aven't I? Leaves twenty-five minutes past midnight unless they've changed the time-table. We can sort out where Don is, go an' 'ave a decent meal, then there will still be time for a couple of drinks before I see you safely back on to the train.'

Emma was saying a silent prayer that all would work out exactly as Tom had said it would.

Tom was delighted as he pulled the car to a halt twenty minutes later and turned the engine off. He was on home ground. He loved seeing the docks in action, hearing the cry of the hungry gulls overhead as they swooped over the ships and cranes that stood so high along the crowded waterfront.

'Daisy, want me t'go and see if Don 'as shown his face today?'

'Thanks all the same, Tom, nice of you to offer, but I think I'll go meself, seeing as how you've been good enough to bring me 'ere. I feel sure Don must 'ave some back pay to come an' if not I'm gonna ask the gaffer about sick pay. They'd tell me if any dues were owing whereas they wouldn't let on to you.'

'OK, but don't 'ang about. If yer can't see him we'll try the pub.'

Daisy tottered along the wharf. She knew exactly where she was going; many's the time she'd been up here to meet Don. She found the offices soon enough but wasn't too sure how she gained entrance.

A big man well into his fifties wearing a flat cap and overalls waved a grimy hand at her. 'Watch where you're stepping, darlin', it ain't safe for ladies around 'ere,' he kindly told her.

Daisy gave him a saucy smile. 'I'm looking for the main office. I can see the building but I can't find me way in.'

'Round the side,' he gestured. 'There's a staircase bin built on, but watch how you go, luv, it's steep and it's rickety.'

'Thanks,' she said, still smiling.

'Anytime, darlin'. Makes me day to see a good-looking lady.'

Having found the staircase, Daisy carefully began to climb, holding on tightly to the wooden handrail. At the very top she paused to stare out over the river. Ships of all kinds were moored on either side of the Thames, some even laying two abreast, taking their turn to either load or unload their cargo.

Unsung heroes were the men and the officers of the Merchant Navy.

She glanced at the wharfside properties. A great number had taken a severe pounding and there were huge empty spaces where warehouses had been razed to the ground during the German raids over London. Nevertheless, this was London, the heart of England, and for all that the Germans had thrown at this city it was still alive and kicking.

Suddenly Daisy grinned to herself. Sam and Emma had meant well but she'd rather die up here than be buried alive down in the country. She looked down over the side of the steps. The large man wearing the flat cap was looking up; he grinned and made the victory sign with two fingers.

I wonder if I met a strange man in North Waltham whether he would pay me compliments and call me darling, she thought. She didn't know and she didn't care, because while she may have had to leave her home in Woolwich, there was no way she was leaving London.

She had almost forgotten what she had

come up this flight of steps for, when a door was pushed open and a bruiser of a man stood in front of her. He wasn't wearing any jacket, the top three buttons of his shirt were undone showing a very hairy chest, his sleeves were rolled up well beyond his elbows and his arms were heavily tattooed.

''Allo, Mrs Gaskin, remember me?' He held out his hand. 'Bill Rogers, union rep.'

'Course, I remember you, yer daft sod.' Daisy laughed. 'Don't I spend 'alf the evening in your arms on the dance floor whenever the firm throws a do?'

'Bin a while, though, ain't it gal? Thought perhaps you'd come on official business, but there's no need; the union will fight Don's corner.'

'As if I'd get mixed up in Don's affairs! Come to that – as if the bugger would let me!'

It was Bill Rogers' turn to laugh. 'Well, why are you 'ere?'

Daisy pulled a face. 'Bill, it's best you don't ask.'

'Don was here earlier on, an' if it's about your Tessa he's already filled us in on that bloody charade. When he left he said he was off to see Jerry Faulkner and that he'd see some of us later over in the pub.'

'Thanks, Bill. Our Tom is down below, got his relations with him up from the country for the day. We've been to see our Tessa and none of us has had a meal today yet, so I'm 'oping the pub can rustle something up for all of us.'

'Sure they will, luv, and I'll be over meself soon as I finish me paperwork. But while we're on our own I want to assure you that Jerry Faulkner *will* be telling the magistrates that the police were barking up the wrong tree when they assumed the goods found in your Tessa's house had been stolen.'

'Oh Bill, I'd sleep a damn sight better tonight if what you've just said could be taken as Gospel.'

'It can, me darlin'. No, don't start crying, just count on it, 'cos if Faulkner was to persist in being a traitor, I promise you he wouldn't ever need to buy another pair of shoes as long as he lives, 'cos not only would he not have any feet on which to put them, he wouldn't have any bleeding legs either. I think the bastard'll get the picture all right when he listens to what some of the men are gonna tell him.'

For once in her life Daisy didn't know what to say. All she managed was, 'It wasn't fair, the way Mr Faulkner let my Tessa down.'

'No, Daisy, it wasn't. Getting your girl and her mates to do his underhand dirty work was bad enough, but then to drop them right in it – no, it ain't on. He'll find out, no worry on that score. You don't treat young women like that. Not and get away with it, yer don't.'

Daisy wiped her eyes with the back of her hand, stood on her toes and kissed Bill's cheek. She couldn't think of any words to say.

'See you later over at the pub,' he said, and then quickly added, 'Mind how you go down those stairs, they ain't very safe.'

'Dear Lord, I'd forgotten about them and these rotten shoes are killing me. I think I'd better take 'em off.'

Bill Rogers stared in disbelief as Daisy leant against the wall and took first one shoe off and then the other. With her handbag and two shoes in one hand, she stood a minute staring at the rickety flight of steps, then placing her free hand on the rail she cautiously put out a foot to begin her descent.

'Here, wait a minute, for Christ's sake,' Bill yelled. 'The way you're going on, yer gonna fall an' break yer bloody neck.'

The pair of them were laughing like a pair

of idiots as Bill came down the stairs with Daisy cradled in his brawny arms as if she were a young child.

'Whereabouts did you leave the car?' Bill managed to ask when they reached the ground.

'If you stop giggling and look ahead, you'll see Tom and his relations standing a few feet in front of you. I bet they'll be thinking we're both mad.'

Tom came running. ''Allo, Bill, our Daisy got you over a barrel, did she? Don't know how she gets away with it.'

'Great to see yer, Tom, about time you and I got together. I've got a nice little offer in the pipeline but now ain't a good time. Where d'yer want me to dump her?'

'Oi, you,' Daisy said, using her forefinger to dig Bill in the chest. 'Not so much of the dumping.'

Tom was just about to call out to Sam but Sam had sussed out the situation and had the back door of the car wide open.

Emma was sitting in one corner and as the men handed Daisy in beside her she put her arm underneath Daisy's legs and lifted them until they were lying across her own lap.

Daisy leaned back and let out a great sigh of relief, 'Oh, that is wonderful, Emma, just what the doctor ordered, bless you,' she said, dropping her shoes down on to the floor.

'Never mind about blessing my wife, my blessed stomach thinks my throat has been cut. One jam doughnut is all I 'ave had to eat since I left North Waltham in the early hours of this morning.' Sam was complaining, loud and clear.

Tom got into the driver's seat, settled himself, then turned to look at the way the two women had made themselves comfortable.

'Sam, do you think we should leave them both there while we get ourselves a slap-up meal?' he asked very seriously.

'Try it,' Emma said with a lot more authority than she usually showed.

'You'd 'ave two of us to deal with,' Daisy quickly announced.

'In that case, I give up. One I can manage, but two, especially the likes of you, is asking too much of any man,' Tom said, his voice full of mock despair as he winked at Sam, turned the key in the lock and started the car.

# Twelve

Sam's prayers had been answered. He had got his wife on to the train and their journey had begun without them hearing the wail of the air-raid siren warning folk that enemy planes were approaching.

Emma had managed to sleep most of the time, her head resting comfortably on Sam's broad chest. He looked at his wristwatch and nudged her gently.

'Come on, Emma, gather your wits about you; we shall be coming in to Basingstoke in about twenty minutes.'

It took a while before Emma was anything like wide awake. She had eased her shoes off as soon as they had got into the carriage, and now she was bending down to put them back on. That done, she looked at Sam and asked, 'When we get off this train, how are we going to get home?'

Sam gave her a wry smile. 'Good question, and my answer is I haven't the faintest idea.

I certainly can't phone Ted Andrews; it will be getting on for three o'clock by the time we get in because the train was well late leaving Waterloo. John said he'd come and get us but I haven't got a number for the farm, and anyway I wouldn't think of disturbing them at this time of night.'

'Didn't there used to be an all-night cab rank near the station?' Emma asked, thinking for the umpteenth time that she would really be glad when they were safely home.

'There used to be a lot of things that have slowly disappeared. We'll just have to take our chances,' Sam answered rather grumpily.

'God, it's cold,' Emma mumbled as she and Sam made their way off the platform twenty minutes later. The weather had certainly changed, proving that summer had finally come to an end. Being so dark made it worse. The couple of lights that were on in the ticket office did little to help and the lights which would normally illuminate the whole of the station were blacked out.

'Hey, hang on, Mr Pearson. You look as if you could be using some help.'

The Canadian accent was easily identified but Sam had to peer into the black darkness to see who had hailed him. He and Emma had been aware that there were Canadian soldiers on the train when they left London, but they had boarded the train using only the front two carriages and he had no knowledge of where their destination was going to be.

With an influx of so many young men into a small community it was only natural that new friendships had been formed and that most of the locals of North Waltham were on speaking terms with many of the troops.

'Morning, Mrs Pearson. Do you folk have transport?'

Emma was too much taken aback to be able to form an answer, but Sam got in quickly, 'No, we don't, soldier.'

The young man laughed. 'My name is Matt. I have the advantage over you, as I know you, Mr Pearson, from watching you at work in your forge. We're all billeted in what I am given to understand is known locally as the Big House, and we're all being picked up at the station. It will probably only be a lorry, but you are both very welcome to a ride.'

'Young man, you are a life saver. The missus and I thought we would have to wait about here until at least seven o'clock, so yes, please, we would appreciate a lift.'

Sam was feeling all at sixes and sevens. If

these military men were stationed in Lionel Trenfield's house then they must be officers. It was so dark he couldn't make out exactly what uniform Matt was wearing, but he was just thankful that they would now be taken home without having to hang about for hours.

Outside the railway station there was enough noise going on to wake the dead. Kit bags and God knows what else were all being slung up into one lorry while the second lorry already seemed to be pretty full with Canadians, who even at this time in the morning were wide-awake and presumably full of life.

Emma's first reaction was, 'What? Me get into that mucky old thing?'

Sam grabbed her arm, none too gently. 'Emma, you've two choices, ride home or walk. And don't be a minute making up your mind because if you are I shall be long gone.'

However, the Canadian soldiers were more tolerant. They cleared a space, found a pile of sacks for Emma to sit on and placed them so that as she sat on the floor she would be able to rest her back against the side of the lorry.

Two soldiers stood on the tail-board ready to grab Emma, two more stood one each side of her, and on the count of three they swung her forward and upwards.

Emma was very relieved when she finally landed safely inside the lorry. She wasn't best pleased because she thought the way she had been almost thrown into the lorry was undignified.

Sam thought it was hilarious.

When the lorry came to a halt at the corner of their cobbled street there were many willing hands to lift Emma down from the lorry and set her safely on her feet.

She felt so stiff, even walking the few yards to their house was an effort. Sam put his key into the front door and stood aside to let Emma go first, straight into the living room, where she plonked herself down in her armchair and let out a sigh of heartfelt thanks, vowing to herself that nothing in this world was going to entice her away from her home ever again. Leaning her head back and closing her eyes, she heard Sam go through to the scullery and when she heard water running she smiled to herself as she thought, thank God, he's filling the kettle. The rattle of teacups as Sam set them out on the table was music to her ears, and then out of the blue she heard him declare, 'Emily's home!'

Emma was up and out of that chair like a

bat out of hell.

Sam was holding a sheet of writing paper and as she watched his lips moving she grew very impatient. 'What is it, Sam? What did you mean – Emily's home?'

'Ssshh,' he said softly, holding a finger to his lips whilst smiling happily. 'Emily is upstairs in bed.'

Emma crossed her arms over her bosom and hugged herself. At the same time she was rocking to and fro on the balls of her feet. All tiredness was forgotten. 'Is that a note from her? Where was it? How come I didn't see it?'

Sam came to her and gently put his arm around her shoulders. 'Come and sit at the table, I'll pour the tea out, then while you're drinking yours I'll read out what Emily has written. I've only glanced through it myself.'

Even the first few sips of the hot tea did a lot to refresh Emma but not half as much as the thought that both of her daughters were home under the same roof, actually tucked up safely in bed. Dear God, thank you, she said to herself.

'Right, here we go.' Sam drained the rest of his tea and set the cup down on to the saucer. Then he picked up the single sheet of notepaper and straightened it out.

Emma was thinking: 'If you are going through all of these motions just to tantalize me than you're doing a good job, Sam, but I will not let on that the wait is sheer torture; I'm just focusing on the fact that our Emily is home.'

'Ready?' Sam finally asked

*Sam Pearson, you are pushing your luck too far; one more delay, just one, and I won't be responsible for my actions.* Emma merely nodded her head.

*Dear Mum & Dad,*

*I was given the task of driving a high-ranking officer to Surrey and ordered to leave the car there and travel back to Colchester by train. Having been given travel warrants I also wangled a forty-eight hour pass. So here I am. Couldn't believe that you had both gone to London. Don't worry, Bella cooked me the best dinner I have had in ages. See you in the morning*

*Love you tons, Emily xxx*

Sam's voice had been full of emotion as he had read the note aloud. Emma was crying softly but they were tears of joy. Oh, yes, God was good. Suppose they had stayed at

Daisy's and missed being with Emily! They really were tears of joy.

'Come on, love; let's go and get into bed. We may as well have a few hours sleep,' Sam said in a low whisper as he guided her towards the stairs.

When they reached the top of the stairs, Emma hesitated. 'I'm just going to open the bedroom door. I've got to have a peep, make sure she really is here.'

Sam blocked her way. 'No, Em, let her be. You don't want to wake her, do you?'

'Just a peep,' Emma implored.

'Oh, go on then. I'll hold the door.' Sam hadn't needed too much persuasion to make him agree.

It was a sight that she wouldn't have missed. Emily had thrown the bedcovers back to halfway down the bed, and one bare arm was flung out straight as if she were reaching for someone to hold on to. Her hair was loosely spread over the pillow and seeing how lovely it was, Emma knew why women's hair was often referred to as their crowning glory.

It was half past ten when Emma woke up to the sound of voices. Hastily swinging her legs over the side of the bed she slipped her feet into her slippers but didn't bother to put her dressing gown on.

Emily was sitting up in bed with a cup of tea in her hand, and her father was sitting on the side of her bed. Emily saw her mother standing in the doorway and straight away she put the cup and saucer down on the bedside table, was out of bed in two ticks and had her arms wrapped around her mother. No words were necessary; the warmth and the closeness were enough. Then they heard Bella's voice yelling from downstairs.

'Don't tell me you're all still in bed. There's me been up at the crack of dawn and done a good few hours of back-breaking work.'

Suddenly the little house was rocking with laughter, with hugs and kisses all round, and Sam said, 'I'll cook a slap-up breakfast for all of us.'

Bella said, 'Jack Briggs has given me the rest of the day off and Joyce gave me a dozen newly laid eggs.'

Emily voice was full of light-hearted sarcasm. 'A dozen eggs! God, how you must have suffered because of this war.'

Poor Emma. She couldn't take her eyes off her two girls, so it wasn't until there was a lull in the bantering that she meekly asked, 'Shall I make the toast? Though I don't suppose we've got so much as a scrape of butter left.'

Bella looked at her mother and said, 'Oh, yes, we have, Mum. I've just put some under the stone pot in the scullery.'

Then grinning at her sister, she said, 'I did a Tom this morning. I came through the dairy where Joyce was patting and rolling butter, and she edged a nice lump towards me and said, you can tell Emily that you found it before it was lost.'

It took a minute or two for the parents to grasp what Bella had said, but then the laughter erupted once again.

Eventually the four of them sat down to a breakfast cooked by their father. It was a meal which wouldn't have been a disgrace if served up to the King and Queen.

The question had to be asked: how long had Emily got?

'I have to report in at Colchester Driving Pool by nine o'clock on Thursday morning,' Emily dolefully told them.

'But it's Tuesday today,' her mother protested.

'Yes, I know, doesn't give me long. But, Mum, let's look on it as a bonus.'

'You'll be travelling tomorrow,' her father said knowingly.

'Afraid so. Really early. But it was worth it,

Dad, if only to eat your wonderful breakfast.'

'Oh, never mind that you were glad to see us or that I scrounged around and cooked you a dinner last night – Dad's breakfast gets the trophy.' Bella pretended she was hurt.

Emma thought, Here we go again; it's a joy to listen to them and hear them argue on matters that aren't in any way serious. This is the way family life should be. Oh, if only this damn war would come to an end...

Bella looked at her mother. She seemed so tired; in fact, she looked washed out. 'Mum, how did things go in London?' she asked, but not waiting for an answer, she went on. 'It's obvious Daisy didn't want to come and stay with us.'

'It wasn't as simple as that,' her mother retorted sharply, then, unable to contain herself any longer, she blurted out, 'The whole family have so much on their plate at the moment that they decided it was best if they stayed together. Though to be honest, I don't think Daisy would have come if you'd have offered her a big gold clock. Living in the country is like being buried alive, according to Daisy's way of thinking. I think Tom had put her off a bit.'

At the mention of Tom's name, Bella felt her cheeks flush and hoped that nobody else would notice. She took a deep breath before asking, 'Did you get to see anything of Tom?'

'Yes, luv, we did, quite a lot. Yesterday we spent most of the day with him.'

'How was he?'

'Fighting fit, cocky as ever, still *doing deals* as he puts it.'

'That sounds like our Tom,' Emily said, laughing.

'Do *you* see much of Tom these days?' Bella asked her sister.

'I suppose I do one way or another, or perhaps I should say I did because I won't be able to see so much of him now I'm stuck up in Colchester.'

'Emily, have you got any washing or mending you'd like me to do while you're here?' Emma asked her eldest daughter, her motherly instinct coming to the fore as usual.

'No ... well, only a couple of pairs of briefs; everything else will be fine until I get back to barracks.'

'Well, go upstairs and fetch them down. I'm going to do our washing this afternoon, get rid of all that London grime. You should have seen the collar of your father's shirt when he took it off after we got home – talk about a dirty tidemark.'

'So, Mum, you think even the air is different in London, do you?' Bella said, teasing her.

'I don't think, I ruddy well know it is. What with all the brick dust from the demolition, and smoke from the factory chimneys, not to mention that nigh on every person you speak to smokes like they've got their own chimney on top of their head, it's a wonder they don't all die from the pollution.'

Bella laughed. 'Mum, you sounded as if you thought that Daisy was paranoid when it came to her living in the country. If she could have heard what you've just said about London, I think she'd say the same about you.'

'Yeah, well, it takes all sorts. Are you two girls going to waste the afternoon or are you going for a walk?'

'That's an idea,' Emily said, glancing at Bella. 'Have you got any sweet coupons left for this month?'

'No, sorry. I usually buy the four-week ration in one go, eat them in a week and have to go without for the next three weeks.' Then a sudden thought came to Bella. 'We could call in and see Joe and Lucy Cadman. When they get hold of sugar they sometimes make their own boiled sweets and they might let you have a few.'

'Great, it's mainly for the train journey I like a sweet to suck, though it never bothers me when I'm driving.'

Bella giggled. 'We could always call in at the farm. I'll dig you up some young carrots, Mum will scrape them, and you can sit on the train and nibble those.'

The two sisters had left most of the houses behind, and were now walking where the grass was green and the trees leafy. When the 'Big House' came into view, Bella said, 'Bit different up there now. No dances or fêtes allowed; all that sort of thing has to be held in the church hall.'

'Military taken it over completely, have they?' Emily asked.

'Suppose so.' Bella shrugged. 'I know Mr and Mrs Trenfield moved out some time ago; they live in a cottage on the estate now. They seem happy enough, always speak when I see them in the village, and they both seem very alert, always willing to take part in any village activity.' Bella pointed a finger and nodded her head. 'Sleeping quarters and what-have-you for the rank and file have all been erected way over in the woods. Mainly it's officers that stay in the house –

well, that seems to be the general idea.'

'Do the military personnel mix with the villagers?' It was a long time since Emily had been home and she now felt she was out of touch.

'In the main I think they do. If we meet up with them in the pub or at a social gathering they do seem pleased to have ordinary folk to talk to,' Bella told her.

'Daft, isn't it? They're all far away from their homes and their loved ones,' Emily remarked with feeling. Then she went on to a different track. 'How about when Tom comes home? Does he get on all right with the Americans and the Canadians?'

'Tom gets on with everybody, you know that well enough, Emily, unless they decide to tread on his toes.'

'Bella, do you have feelings for our Tom?' Emily cautiously asked.

'Of course I do, have done from the moment he stepped into our house with John all those years ago. You too have feelings for him, don't you, Emily?'

Emily sighed softly. 'Tell me to stop if you think I am interfering, but I just happened to note how you looked when you asked Mum about him. Are your feelings different, kind of serious?'

'Oh, Emily, what's the use? I am glad to talk to you about him.' She paused and sighed softly but heavily. 'But Tom is kind of our brother! You know how old-fashioned Mum and Dad are, and most of our friends and neighbours. They look on us as a family, and so did I, until one night when he took me dancing. We hadn't been off the floor for about four dances and we were both whacked out. I kind of fell into his arms and he kissed me. He'd kissed me many times before, like he has you, but only the once like that.' Bella stared at her sister then suddenly her whole body sagged. Lowering her head, she murmured, 'Oh, Emily, isn't this awful? I never meant it to happen. I always looked forward to Tom coming home, and now I really want him to come and yet I feel I should tell him to stay away. If you want me to tell you the truth, I not only love Tom I am in love with him, for all the good it will do me. I daren't let him know how I feel about him. He's got everything going for him – he's good-looking, charming, always dressed so smartly, he can have the pick of any girls – why would he look at me?'

Emily was at a loss as to what to say. She looked lovingly at her sister.

'Are you sure that Tom is the one man you

really want?' she asked her bluntly.

'Oh, Emily, I have never been more certain of anything; I have tried going out with other fellows but the whole time I'm uneasy, comparing what they say and how they act with Tom. But with Tom, I am so completely happy, even if we only go for a walk, it makes my heart sing just to be with him and have him hold my hand.'

They came to the village green and just naturally walked to the seat that was fixed to the bottom of the trunk of the big oak tree. There they sat down side by side as they had done many times during the years they had been growing up together.

It was Emily that broke the silence. 'Bella dear, have you given any thought to what might happen when this war is finally over?'

Bella made no comment, just continued to stare at the small white daisies that sprinkled the green grass.

'Listen to me, Bella, life in this village is the only life you've ever known. It has been everything you have loved, all you have ever wanted, until now. Have you given any thought as to how different Tom is? He has never known complete security, what he has he has worked for, and he's a true London lad, a street lad you might say, because he certainly knows his way around and can quite easily take care of himself.

'He is more than proud to admit that we are his family, and I am one hundred per cent sure, that if it came to it, he would gladly lay down his life for Mum, Dad, you or me, without so much as a moment's hesitation. There's nothing to say that he won't suddenly realize that he can love you in a different way than merely loving you as a sort of sister. You've come round to that way of thinking, so who's to say that Tom won't be utterly thrilled when he wakes up to the fact that his little Bella is now a truly lovely grown-up young lady?'

Silent tears were trickling down Bella's cheeks, but she smiled a little and held up her hands, showing her chipped and broken fingernails. 'I'm a land girl. Will he love me, calluses an' all?'

Emily tried hard to lighten the atmosphere. 'Who knows? We may yet live to see you two married with half a dozen children, and Tom either being the best farmer in the village or taking over the smithy from Dad and shoeing the horses that belong to the local gentry.'

'Yeah, and when the army no longer has need of your services, my dear sister you should think seriously of becoming an author. I am sure the fairy stories you could turn out would automatically become bestsellers.'

They were both laughing as they held each other close.

Emily hadn't been able to give Bella much advice but she had certainly helped her to look on the bright side.

It must be true what they say, Bella thought, a trouble shared is a trouble halved.

# Thirteen

Emily paid off the taxi and looked up at the clock tower; it was five minutes to four. She picked up her suitcase from the pavement where the driver had placed it and walked through the gates of Colchester Barracks. Quite suddenly, she felt very vulnerable and terribly lonely. Since her transfer to Colchester she hadn't had time to settle in and she hadn't made any friends. Now a long lonely evening stretched out in front of her.

First she had to report to the duty officer

and get herself signed in. Having gone through all the motions she saluted the officer and was about to leave when a young recruit, who was sitting at a writing desk in the far corner of the room, called out, 'Corporal Pearson, I have a message for you.'

Emily did a quick turn-about, and took a few steps until she was standing facing the girl who, though she was wearing ATS uniform, looked no more than about fifteen years old.

She was busy sorting through a hefty great pile of forms. 'Give me a minute please, Corporal,' she said, without looking up.

All Emily wanted to do was to take her clothes off and lie in a nice hot bath, but she stood patiently waiting until at last the girl murmured, 'Great, that's that lot finished.' Then she lifted her head and smiled; her hair had been cut quite short but a straight fringe had been left that lay across her forehead. Now Emily thought she looked even younger, straight out of the schoolroom. Surely the War Office wasn't that desperate for recruits, she reflected.

'There is a note here for you, Corporal. A gentleman brought it in soon after I came on duty.'

Emily said, 'Thank you,' and accepted the envelope. Then once again she picked up her suitcase and left the gatehouse.

There were just four beds in the room that had been allocated to Emily but so far in the short time that she had been there, there had ever only been one other occupant besides herself, a friendly, chatty girl by the name of Laura Evans, about the same age as herself. There was no sign of Laura except that a copy of today's *Daily Mirror* lay open on her bed. At least Laura is still here, Emily told herself as she began to take off her uniform and to hang it in the narrow wardrobe that stood beside her bed. Having put on a cotton housecoat she sat down on her bed and using her thumb nail she slit open the envelope that was addressed to Corporal Emily Pearson. She pondered on that fact for a moment. It wasn't the usual form of address that the army would use; it was much more personal.

Well, you won't know who has written to you unless you read the letter, she scolded herself.

*Dear Corporal Pearson,*
*I understand that you have been assigned to be my driver while I am in Colchester.*

*Your name was familiar to me. It appears
that you and I both hail from the Hampshire village of North Waltham.*

*I shall be in the bar of the mess hall at
six p.m. If you are free at that time I
would very much like you to join me for a
drink.*

*Richard Trenfield*

Emily found her thoughts wandering in
many different directions. Of course the
name Trenfield was familiar to her and she
had known that Mr and Mrs Trenfield had
three sons, two that lived abroad, and
Richard whom she had known of for as long
as she could remember, but it was ages since
she had seen him. Certainly their paths had
not crossed since war had been declared.
During the years she was at school she
recalled Richard Trenfield paying regular
visits to his parents, and whenever a fête or a
charity do took place in the village he would
always be there, anxious to help.

When she and Bella were out walking they
would sometimes see him and he would
always stop and speak to them. Emma and
Sam told them they should always address
him as Mister Richard.

Three times Emily read the note. It wasn't

an order, since Mr Trenfield wasn't military personnel; in fact, she was totally ignorant as to what exactly he was doing here in Colchester. But there, she sighed, mine is not to question why; I'll go and meet him if only to satisfy my curiosity.

She lay on the bed reading Laura's newspaper for about half an hour, then she got up and showered, all the time wondering what she should wear that would be appropriate for this meeting. She really did not want to have to put her uniform back on, but what else had she? Her choice was pretty limited. Finally she settled on a very pale green linen suit, knowing the colour brought out the glints in her glossy chestnut hair. The suit wasn't very warm but she supposed that she would only be having the one drink in the mess. Her one and only pair of high-heeled shoes were black, but she had a choice of earrings and chose the tiny pearl studs her parents had brought her for her last birthday. It felt good to dress up for a change.

It was a few minutes after six when Emily walked into the mess and saw that Richard Trenfield had arrived. He had been standing at the bar but had obviously been watching for her because he immediately put his drink down and came towards her, with a broad smile and hand outstretched. 'Thank you for coming, Corporal. Quite a coincidence, wouldn't you say? But come, let's get you seated.'

Although Emily was unaware of it herself, she had made a stunning impression and several heads turned as she walked to the table.

'I'll fetch you a drink and then we can talk. What will you have?'

'A dry white wine, please, sir.' Emily had difficulty in saying the words as Richard pulled a chair out from a table and held it while she sat down. Not the least of her worries was how she was supposed to address this man. As he walked towards the bar Emily let out a great gasp of air, thankful for the respite.

She couldn't believe this was happening. He was nothing like the Mister Richard that she remembered. Although he visited his parents frequently it had been years since she'd spoken to him, not since she was a child. He was wearing a charcoal-grey double-breasted suit, a sparkling white shirt and a maroon tie. He was tall, well-built, a very handsome man with a thick head of light brown hair and blue eyes. She lifted her head and really stared at the back of him as he stood at the bar. There was an athletic look to him – must be the broad shoulders, she decided. He was almost too good looking, though not in any way like Clive Beaumont who was brash, but he had an air of cool dignity.

It was Richard that brought the subject up the minute he had set their drinks down on the table. 'Difficult to know how to address one another,' he said, smiling. 'I know a little of what has been happening to you, Emily, I get the news from my parents when I go home. They keep tabs on youngsters who have joined up, at least where it's possible. I did learn that you had been injured in an air raid. You deserved your promotion. Are you fully recovered now?'

'Yes, thank you, sir. I've had sick leave but am now passed fit for duty.'

Richard took a drink from his glass of beer and drew himself up straight.

'This is ridiculous,' he murmured. 'I've known you since the day you were born. You do not have to address me as sir, and I refuse to keep calling you corporal.'

His words were like setting a match to a tinderbox. They looked at each other and in seconds were both laughing like a couple of children who had just been let out from school.

It took a minute or two for Emily to stop giggling and when she had, she said, 'I think the rules will have to be applied whilst I am your driver, sir.'

That set them off again. This time it was Richard that said, 'Emily, you have not touched your drink. Take a few sips, see if it is to your liking, and for the rest of this evening we shall only use our Christian names, agreed?'

'Agreed.' Emily smiled cautiously. 'But I think I should go when I have finished my drink, as I have to be on duty early in the morning.'

Richard's face was stern as he answered. 'Actually, I was hoping you'd have dinner with me. We can still make it an early night.'

Emily hesitated for a couple of minutes. She was tempted. It had been a rough tiring journey and she hadn't had a proper meal all day, but what if her commanding officer got wind of it?

'I don't think that would be permissible. I'm sorry.'

He leaned forward and took her hand. 'If I go back to my room I shall spend the whole evening worrying about the coming

161

week, which is a rather important one for me, so much so that I shall go crazy. Please, Emily, keep me company. I would appreciate it.'

He sounded very sincere and perhaps a little lonely.

'I'm not sure that I will be doing the right thing, but maybe we could make it early – I don't have a late pass.'

He laughed. 'I promise you won't have to gain entry by climbing over the wall. I'll have you back here in good time.'

'I shall have to fetch a wrap from my room; I didn't think I would be leaving the barracks.'

'That's all right; give me time to ask the staff sergeant if he can recommend a decent restaurant, as I'm not familiar with this part of the world. I'll be waiting for you when you're ready.'

Fifteen minutes later, as promised, he was waiting for her. He took her arm and linked it through his own before they started to walk towards the gatehouse. He had arranged for a taxi to take them to the Trident Restaurant, which the sergeant had assured him was as good as any you would find these days.

The taxi was waiting outside. It was only a

short journey, and Richard paid the cabby and asked him to come back for them at nine thirty. Giving him a large tip ensured that he would willingly do so.

Inside they were shown to a quiet corner table. Richard asked if there was a speciality for the day on the menu and on being told that the chef had been able to obtain a few Dover soles, he looked at Emily, raised his eyebrows in question and, when she smilingly agreed, he ordered the fish for them both and asked to see the wine list.

Then he turned to her and asked her a question she hadn't expected.

'Tell me about Tom Yates; did your parents ever legally adopt him?'

'No, they didn't, but it wasn't for want of trying. We have always looked upon Tom as very much a part of our family.'

'I know he gets down to see your folks whenever he can, but do you see much of him, Emily?'

'I have done whilst I've been stationed in London, but now – ' she shrugged her shoulders – 'who knows?' Then as an afterthought she asked, 'How come you seem to know about Tom?'

'My parents have retained a great interest in several of the children who first came to stay with families in the village courtesy of the Toc H. My mother loves to write and receive letters. She continues to correspond with a couple of those children even after all these years.'

Emily wasn't satisfied. 'You haven't answered my question.'

'Every resident of North Waltham remembers Tom Yates and John Kirby. They took those two boys to their hearts and the whole village mourned the death of John; he was so young.'

'Yes, he was,' Emma said, feeling a lump rising in her throat. 'There will never be another young man like him.'

She refrained from saying, *Well, not for me anyway*.

Richard immediately sensed that the loss of John had greatly affected Emily and so he quickly changed the subject. 'My father had a soft spot for Tom, he still has.' He broke off and grinned widely. 'I think all the time this war continues he will remain in Tom's debt.' Richard saw that Emily was looking at him in a strange way, and with a saucy wink he added, 'My father likes a drop of good scotch before he retires at night.'

'Really!' Emily exclaimed as the penny dropped. 'I didn't think our Tom's activities reached as far as dealing with Mr Trenfield.'

'As I'm sure you know Emily, my parents no longer reside in what you call the Big House. They're safely tucked up in a small bungalow and they tell me they receive far more visitors there than they ever did at the house, so I don't think they will be in a hurry to take up residence again when the war is over.'

'When?' Emily exclaimed, sighing. 'Do you get down to see them often?'

'Not as often as I would like. When we led normal lives I always made sure that I took the whole of August off to be with them.' He paused, as the waiter brought their wine, poured a little for Richard's approval and at his nod poured them each a full glass. When they both had taken a drink, Richard gave Emily a grin. 'I well remember you and your sister Arabella dancing around the maypole.'

Emily gasped with surprise.

Before she had thought of an answer he said, 'In those far off days the whole village had great fun even if we did get dirty in the process.'

'I bet you never got dirty!' Her hand shot to cover her mouth, she hadn't meant to say that out loud and, which made it more embarrassing, at that moment the waiter brought their meal to the table.

Richard laughed uproariously. 'Well, you'd lose your bet. I often looked a right mess, what with the things I did for charity.'

Emily couldn't imagine it. Her memory of him was of a well-dressed, posh gentleman. Now he seemed hungry to know more about her and by now she was comfortable talking to him. And, at least for one whole week, they were going to see a lot of each other. There didn't seem any harm in really getting to know each other.

The fish and the fresh vegetables that were served with it were delicious and the chef's sauce had a wonderful lemony tang. With a smile of satisfaction they laid their knives and forks down. Almost immediately the waiter appeared again and offered a choice of sweets.

'No, nothing more for me,' Emily said, patting her tummy, 'but that was a really nice meal. Thank you, Richard.'

'At least share a pot of coffee with me; we have time before the taxi arrives,' Richard insisted.

The coffee was brought in a pot together with a jug of hot milk, which Emily thought was excellent. So often these days all you were offered was a cup of coffee, with no preference as to how much milk or cream you liked with it.

The taxi arrived, and in no time at all they were back at the barracks and were walking towards the gatehouse. Emily excused herself while she entered and signed herself in.

'Thank you again, Richard; I have had a most enjoyable evening,' Emily told him with true feeling as they reached the main door to her quarters.

'Me too. I am grateful that you rescued me,' he said. 'Will you be all right?'

'I think I can manage,' she said and grinned at him. 'You get a good night's sleep. I'll see you in the morning.'

'I'll be there at eight thirty,' he promised. 'Maybe we can have another meal together sometime. We have so much more still to talk about.'

'Let's see how your work schedules pan out,' she said sensibly, closing the door quietly behind her.

She was amazed to find Laura not only in bed but fast asleep. She must have been tired, Emily told herself, nevertheless she was pleased she would be able to get into bed and go over everything in her mind that she and Richard had said and told each other during the course of the evening,

It certainly was a turn-up for the books. This time yesterday she was at home with her family and now ,a good many miles from her home, she had just had a wonderful meal with the son of Mr Trenfield who owned the largest property and the most land in the village where she had been born.

Sometimes it did seem as if it were a small world.

# Fourteen

Next morning, there was a spring to Emily's step as she collected her duty forms and rota for the day before making for the motor pool. Having signed her allotted car out, she checked the fuel gauge and set the driving seat back a little before heading for the pick-up point.

Richard Trenfield was waiting and immediately she caught sight of him her heart was pounding against her ribs. He looked even more handsome in the daylight; his navy blue pin-striped suit, blue shirt and navy tie showed his good taste as did his well-polished black leather shoes. He was holding a black briefcase and tucked under his arm were several thick folders.

*Why are you letting him affect you so much?* she asked herself and at the same time muttered, 'Silly question.' Probably because in her everyday life it was uniforms and more uniforms. To see such a well-turned-out gentleman at this time in the morning was indeed a rarity.

They chatted comfortably for a minute or two until he stated his preference for sitting in the back of the car. Emily stepped forward and opened the rear door and as she did so Richard dropped his folders. Simultaneously they bent to retrieve them, their heads banged together and he let go of his briefcase.

Emily straightened her driver's cap and bit her tongue. What she would have liked to say was: *Oh, for God's sake, just get in the car and leave me to deal with all these papers.* What she did say as she handed him his briefcase was, 'Sorry, sir, we shall have your papers tidy in no time.'

Two girls from the office had rushed out and already most of the papers were placed inside a folder. Whether the right papers were in the right folder she wouldn't have liked to guess.

It was a silent journey. Richard had the whole of the back seat on which to sort his work into the correct order.

It was forty-five minutes later when Emily checked her route map and knew she was approaching Maplehurst Hall. Less than a mile further on, she turned the car into a driveway with tall hedges on either side. Gates opened automatically and she drove through and was soon looking at a huge, handsome stone house, with a large area of lawn on either side, several beautiful old trees, and an attractive pond with an ornamental fountain placed in the centre. It was an idyllic scene, and in total contrast to war-torn London, she thought as she brought the car to a halt.

Several men, all wearing good suits, were standing at the foot of the stone steps that led up to the main front door which was wide open. In the open doorway a smart-looking woman in her late forties stood watching them and Emily supposed her to be the housekeeper because the costume she was wearing was black, and her white blouse had a stiff stand-up collar.

From the little knowledge that she had gathered about the gentlemen that she drove for, quite a few were attached to the Home Office in Whitehall, though some time ago she had spent a week driving for a gentleman whose office had been in Whitechapel. God, that had been awful. The whole district had suffered so heavily from German bombs that most streets had been impassable. As she took another quick look around she felt she could be forgiven for thinking that today she was in a different world.

She turned to look at Richard and was rewarded by a lovely smile.

'Sorry about the chaos earlier,' he said.

'All in a day's work,' she answered lightly. Then without intending to she caught herself saying, 'What a lovely spot in which to spend your day.'

'We are here to work,' he stiffly reminded her. Then he seemed to sense that he had been a bit sharp and added, 'You have a good day.'

'I will,' she told him brightly.

'I wish I could believe that,' he said apologetically.

Emily chose not to answer; instead she said, 'My instructions don't give a pick-up time.'

'No, we have to have some leeway. It is not even definite that I shall be returning to

Colchester tonight, it depends entirely how the meetings progress, but you will be kept informed.' Then very hesitantly he lowered his voice and said, 'Goodbye, Emily, I shall look forward to our next meeting.'

His words shocked her, as she had been under the impression that she was to be attached to him for seven days. And another thing – when he said, 'Goodbye, Emily,' he had used her Christian name. Old habits die hard.

Richard leaned into the car and fetched out his briefcase. Emily gathered the folders safely together and handed them to him. Then almost mechanically she drew herself to attention and saluted him.

'Thank you, sir,' was all she was able to say.

It was a very despondent Emily that got back into her car; she lay back against the seat and closed her eyes. Her thoughts were all of Richard Trenfield. She wondered if he were married, trying to imagine the kind of woman he would be drawn to. She had never heard that he was married, so perhaps he wasn't. Another question popped up – how old did she think he was?

'I'm not very good on ages,' she said aloud, and then she laughed. He had to be twelve years older than she was, maybe more, but because he looked so good it was difficult to tell. She had to pull herself together: this was ridiculous – what had any of it to do with her?

Yet during the whole hour that it took her to drive back to base her thoughts were of him.

Checking with the duty officer, she was told she had two pick-ups for the afternoon but until then she was free. Emily looked at her watch; lunch wasn't such a bad idea and as it was still early a cup of coffee beforehand would be rather nice, she decided.

She made for her room, washed her hands, changed her shoes and combed her hair. The first person she saw as she walked into the mess was Clive Beaumont.

'Oh, hell,' she said aloud, since he was the last person that she wanted to see. She was about to turn and hurry away when he came striding towards her.

'What are you doing tonight, Emily?' he asked, taking her arm and steering her towards the bar.

'What am I doing?' she asked. 'I don't rightly know until I get issued with my orders. Maybe having an early night,' she said, hoping to put him off.

'Would you like me to take you out for

something to eat?'

She couldn't believe what she was hearing. He was acting as though the incident in the pub at Rye had never happened and as though he was doing her a kindness in offering to take her out.

He saw the look of distrust on her face and he had the grace to say, 'I know I owe you an apology, so let me make it up to you.'

'Thank you for asking, Clive,' Emily said, doing her best to be polite, 'but if you don't mind I'll give it a miss tonight.'

'Well, at least let's eat together now. Do you want to stay here or go somewhere else?'

'I am not allowed to leave base until I know what my orders are, as I may well have to go back to pick a client up.'

'That's settled then – shall we sit over there?' he said, pointing to where there were several vacant tables.

He was certainly very attentive today, Emily thought, as she wondered why he was not in uniform. In fact, he was dressed very casually, in well-cut brown trousers and a fawn open-necked shirt; it might be sunny outside but it was weak sunshine and the wind was quite cold.

'Bit early to eat, would you like a drink or some coffee maybe?' he invited.

'Thank you, some coffee would be fine,' she told him, still wondering why he was being so nice.

Clive actually carried the two cups of coffee to their table, enquiring as he did whether she took sugar.

'No, I don't, just as it is will be fine.'

'Just as well, because I've just heard Alan say that until supplies arrive all they can offer are saccharine tablets.'

'Horrible sickly sweet things,' Emily said, pulling a face.

'Would you like a look at a newspaper?' Clive suggested. 'There are still a few in the rack.'

'Thanks, Clive; it's not often we get a chance to sit and scan the news in peace.'

For the next thirty minutes they sat in companionable silence, each reading a paper, until Clive handed her a menu.

'Your thoughts the same as mine?' he asked, as he watched Emily wrinkle her nose. 'What the menu offers and what the mess can provide are often two entirely different things.'

'They usually have a good selection of salads,' Emily said hopefully.

'Is that all you want, salad? You must have something to go with it.'

'Well, how about a jacket potato? That will suit me fine.'

Clive went to place their order and when he came back he didn't look too pleased. 'Only two other choices apart from the usual rabbit food – macaroni cheese or corned beef rissoles,' he groaned.

'What have you chosen?' Emily enquired out of politeness.

'Macaroni. I can just about stand corned beef in a sandwich if I am hungry enough, but heated up it becomes revolting.'

'So for you it was Hobson's Choice?'

'Yes, you could say that,' he agreed, giving Emily a long-suffering look.

They were halfway through their meal when Clive suddenly said, 'Emily, you are a right party pooper.'

Emily spluttered, her mouth full of butter-ed potato. 'How the hell do you make that out?' she demanded.

'That half-wit that you allow to take you out and about. You could do so much better for yourself, but you never will, not while you tag along with him.'

Emily clenched her fists until her finger-nails were digging into the palms of her hands. She knew that he was referring to Tom. 'What gives you the right to refer to

Tom as a half-wit? I gather it *is* Tom you are referring to?'

Emily was angry and it showed.

'Well, yes, I know him as Tom because I've heard you use his name when I've met you at the Rainbow Rooms in Piccadilly. He's a good dancer, I'll give you that, but that's about all he's got going for him.'

'Oh, and that's your own opinion, is it?'

'I'm sorry if I have offended you, Emily, but I've no time for wallies like him, men that have never put a uniform on.'

Emily had to count to ten and also take a deep breath before she could bring herself to answer him.

'Oh, and shall I tell you, Clive, his opinion of you is no better. He once asked me what you were captain of – what was it, Dad's Army? And did you parade with broom handles because you had never been issued with proper guns.'

The minute she let the words out she knew she had gone too far. Clive looked as if he were about to explode.

Minutes went by and neither of them moved, not to eat, drink, or to utter one single word. Then eventually, Emily thought it best that she be the peacemaker.

'Captain Beaumont,' she began, which

immediately had him giving her his full attention. 'I shall tell you all you need to know about Tom, and then it will be your turn. First, Tom is my brother.' She waited a few minutes to allow that piece of information to sink in, not in the least bit worried that it was not strictly true.

'Secondly, he has worked in Woolwich Arsenal since he was fifteen years old. Before the war started he was quite sure that eventually England was going to declare war with Germany and he volunteered for every branch of the services. He even tried the Merchant Navy. But because of his work and his knowledge of munitions he was classed as being exempt from serving in any branch of the armed forces. That was not to say that he was given a free choice. He had to stay in his present employment whether he wanted to or not.'

Emily was just thinking you could have cut the air with a knife, when Clive reached out and caught hold of her hand.

'I am sorry, Emily,' he said with difficulty, almost as if the words were choking him.

Emily was not so sure that his apology was entirely sincere.

She was about to prompt him when he said, 'During my last year at university I became ill and was found to be suffering from consumption; no medication worked for me, I was wasting away. My parents decided to send me to Switzerland, and it worked wonders for me but not one hundred per cent. Hence my only contribution to the war effort is a desk job.'

Now it was Emily's turn to reach for his hand and hold it tightly.

'We have both of us taken life at its face value, haven't we, Emily?' Clive asked, using a tone of voice that was not normal for him. 'We'll do better than that tonight.'

'Now you are taking too much for granted,' she quickly said, though feeling better because at least they had cleared the air. And she hoped that, whether or not they ever got together again, they could be friends from now on.

Later when Emily reported for duty she wasn't at all surprised to be told that Mr Trenfield would not need transport until midday tomorrow. She was kept busy for the remaining hours of Thursday and didn't sign off duty until seven o'clock.

Wonders of wonders, who should be waiting for her but Clive Beaumont.

'Ready for a night at a small club that I happen to be a member of?' he asked as he walked her back to her quarters.

'May I ask you something first, Clive?'

He nodded, and Emily asked 'What are you doing here in Colchester and why are you in civvies all the time?'

'All right, I'll come clean; I'm on leave for fourteen days and I should be elsewhere but I prefer to stay around here.'

'Has this anything to do with the young lady that was with you when we met in Rye?'

'Clever, aren't you? Yes, Tricia is her name and we were engaged for six months before she broke it off.'

Emily was laughing to herself. It was as if a complete change had come over this young man. He wasn't anywhere near so sure of himself any more. 'Do you want her back?' she bravely asked, knowing he would be well within his rights to tell her to mind her own business.

'I honestly don't know, not for sure, that is. Tricia can be a pain in the backside some-times, but financially we both lose out, big time,' he said with a sigh, 'if we don't get married.'

Emily stopped dead in her tracks and she spoke without thinking. 'What you have just said about this Tricia might equally apply to you, and even to consider how you might benefit financially is no reason for two people to decide whether or not they want to get married.'

'Oh, Emily love, why are you so different, so naive? Are you going to tell me that if a vast sum of money was going to be settled on you on condition that you married a certain person you would turn the offer down?'

'If I didn't love the person, of course I would. How can you contemplate living with someone for the rest of your life if you aren't going to really love them?'

'Where have you been all my life, Emily? Playing Happy Families?'

'I suppose you could say that is an apt description of my life so far. My father adores my mother and my mother feels exactly the same way about him. My sister, myself and Tom would do anything in this world for either of them. Money would never come into the equation.'

'Shall we forget we ever started this conversation and get ready for a night out on the town?'

'Are you sure you want to be wasting your time with me?' Emily asked, knowing she was taunting him.

Clive chose to ignore the question, merely saying, 'I'll pick you up in half an hour.'

Which suited Emily fine. It gave her enough time to unwind, take a quick bath and change her clothes.

When Clive came to pick her up, she was wearing a short black dress and high-heeled strappy sandals, it was the only dress she had that would pass for evening wear. She had dressed it up by twisting a scarf around her waist. Her Aunt Agnes had crocheted the scarf for her as a birthday present; it was a very fine weave, the palest shade of blue with silver threads running through it. She was wearing make-up and her hair shone like burnished copper from the vigorous brushing she had given it.

Usually she looked very much the part of an ATS driver, but tonight she looked young and sexy.

'Wow! You've certainly set out to stun me tonight, and you've succeeded; you look very glamorous.'

'Thank you, Clive,' she said, blushing slightly and thinking that it was fun getting dressed up for a change, especially getting out of uniform.

Then she reminded herself: two evenings running, she'd been taken out. Oh, well, she'd make the most of it. Luck such as that didn't come too often.

They chatted easily on the way to the club in the taxi that he'd ordered. No sooner had they arrived, and been shown to a table in an alcove, than he ordered a bottle of wine.

He looked very relaxed as he said, 'Come on, Emily, let's go and dance.'

He took her hand and led her on to the dance floor. It was a good evening. They were laughing and happy and relaxed. He was holding her comfortably in his arms, whether dancing slow or fast, moving perfectly with her, but never letting his hands wander or holding her too close. At no time did she feel uncomfortable with him. And without giving a thought to anything more than friendship, Emily thought she could have easily danced with him all night.

If there was anything not quite right it was the meal.

'Very disappointing,' was the remark that Clive made to the waiter as he cleared their plates away. All he got in way of reply was the ever-ready answer. 'There is a war on!'

At least the club was not short of alcohol and Clive made sure the drinks kept coming.

They stayed at the club until one o'clock in the morning and when the taxi dropped them off Clive told her to stand under a tree and wait a few minutes while he went off to make sure that the guard would turn a blind eye.

Emily faced the truth; she had had far too much to drink and right now she wasn't sure where Clive was taking her.

'Clive, you should have left me at the main door. These quarters are for females only,' she was protesting but only half-heartedly, 'and it's so dark I can't see a thing.'

He took his arm from around her waist and she heard him open a door. 'In here,' he whispered, giving her a slight push, and seconds later he was on his knees and dragging her down on to the floor beside him.

Emily felt around and from the feel of the carpet and the alcoholic smell she guessed they were in the bar. Their faces were so close that their noses touched when they spoke. She could feel the warmth of his breath and she felt a thrill run through her as his arms tightened around her body.

He fiddled with the buttons on the back of her dress and then she felt the cloth tear and he was pushing her dress aside leaving her shoulders bare. His lips were now covering hers, his tongue was way down into her mouth and he had released her breasts from her bra. His fingers found her nipple; he began rubbing slowly until it swelled and hardened. She sighed, grew breathless, and his tongue was once again forcing her mouth open.

Emily twisted her body and shoved him away. This was going too far!

'Emily, what's the matter?' He sounded really angry.

'I hate it when you carry on like this; you're letting things get out of hand.'

She sat up in the darkness, pushing herself away until there was space between them and doing her best to straighten her clothing. She felt awful, she was as much to blame as him, since she hadn't tried to stop him, and she felt she had to say something.

'I hate it like this. We've both of us had far too much to drink,' she said. 'It's sleazy.'

'I haven't heard you complain before,' he told her mockingly.

'Before was different. Once, just the once, but at least it was in a bed in a hotel and even then we neither of us thought it was a remarkable success.'

'Suddenly you don't fancy me, is that it?'

'Perhaps. Certainly not rolling about on the floor in a smelly bar. Anyhow...'

'Anyhow what?'

'Anyhow, you said you're going to marry Tricia. So what am I supposed to be?'

Emily's voice had reached a high pitch.

'Of course I shall have to marry Tricia, eventually. I've told you why. But I shall be well off, still able to keep you in a manner that you've never been accustomed to. What's wrong with that?'

Clive felt the sheer weight of Emily's anger. Even her body language, as she pushed him further away and got to her feet. If she had had something heavy in her hand she would have clouted him with it, she felt that aggressive. The truth had only just hit her. To Captain Beaumont, she was a bit of rough! Someone to keep on the side! He had no respect for her. Never had had.

She wished she had never got involved with this creep.

She couldn't have said how she found her room but she did and without too much difficulty. Total surprise hit her when she turned on the light to see that Laura's bed was a mess, the pillows lying on the floor, the covers tangled together in a jumble. There was no sign of Laura, and Emily hoped that she was all right.

It took a long time for her to get herself washed and ready for bed. Finally, when she lay down and her head touched the pillow and the room began to spin round, she made a resolution. 'I'm going to sign a pledge. I am never ever going to drink so much booze again.'

# Fifteen

The days had passed far too quickly. It was now Saturday morning and Emily had been told that her duties with Mr Trenfield would finish today.

They were on their way to Maplehurst House for the last trip and this morning Richard had got into the front passenger seat. He hadn't commented as he got into the car and Emily didn't feel she should remark on what was after all his decision.

This was the fourth time she had made this journey with him, and during each trip they had formed a comfortable friendly relation-ship, though when Emily looked back on the night that he had taken her out for dinner she felt a little disappointed that it had been the one and only time that they had spent time together other than when she was the driver and he was the client.

She was loath to part from him. Just being near him made her feel so good.

The silence between them now was hanging heavily when without warning Richard said, 'I'd like us to meet somewhere away from the barracks when and if you can get leave.'

The words sounded wonderful. Emily was pleased, but she wondered exactly what was he suggesting.

'You make it sound so simple, and we both know it wouldn't be,' she said.

'If one wants something badly enough there is always a way. It is what I want,' he said honestly. He paused. 'Is it what you want, Emily?' he asked her bluntly.

'I don't know what I want, Richard,' she said, being equally honest.

'Have you given any thought as to where you would like to live and what you would prefer to do when this war is finally over?'

'Yes, I have,' she said. 'At the moment my thoughts are all on going home. I have seen a lot of this country including most of London, but not one place has had a lasting effect on me.'

'Early on Monday I am flying to Scotland, that much I can tell you,' Richard said, 'but I am free for the whole of tomorrow. I wondered whether you would like to go for a walk out in the country somewhere, and grab a bite of lunch at some farmhouse or small out-of-the-way café, rather than get all dressed up tomorrow evening. Have you any objections?'

Emily was overwhelmed for a moment as she thought about his suggestion. 'I'd love that,' she said, and she meant it, thinking it would make a really nice change.

But at ten thirty next morning, Richard still looked like an advertisement for a high-class tailoring magazine. He was wearing fawn trousers, a beige shirt with the sleeves rolled up and well-polished shoes. He was carrying a blazer over his shoulder.

Emily looked young and countrified in a navy blue straight skirt and jumper with an Aran cardigan draped around her shoulders. Her shoes were army issue, stout lace-up brogues. Without thinking she said, 'When was the last time you looked a mess, Richard?'

He laughed heartily. 'When I was apple-bobbing at our village annual fête. I slipped and my head and shoulders went into the barrel of water which wasn't very clean.'

Emily was trying to visualize the scene; the

memory had her feeling nostalgic and all at once she was yearning to be at home.

Richard sensed that he had revived memories of happy times of so long ago.

He put out his hand and took hers saying, 'How about we take a bus to get us out of town?'

She looked at him, complete surprise showing plainly on her face. 'Fancy slumming it today, do you?'

'Why not,' he said, laughing. 'We don't use a car very much when we are in Hampshire, do we?'

'In my case that was probably because no one in the family had a car though it will be different now when we get back to normal living,' she said, wistfully.

'So is it to be the top deck of a bus?' Richard asked. 'I've made sure that I have plenty of pennies ready for our fare.'

They both grinned and started to walk out of the barracks, holding hands and talking, like the friends they were rapidly becoming. They did indeed climb the stairs to sit on the top deck of the first bus that came along and the conductor told them that a fourpenny ticket each would take them as far as the bus was going. Emily pulled a scarf out from her handbag and tied it over her head because the wind was fierce and none too warm.

Richard in turn took her hand and placed it into the pocket of his blazer but still kept a tight hold of it. 'I think perhaps we may have been a little too optimistic regarding the weather; after all it is the second week in October and we have to start thinking about the winter.'

They got off the bus at the end of the line and agreed the area looked very nice. Hardly any houses, no shops, just fields, hedges and trees. They walked and talked, and the whole time Richard held on to her hand.

As the sky clouded over they found a pub that looked so good they each said they wished they had a camera with them. The setting was the type of picture that used to feature on expensive boxes of hand-made chocolates. The hanging baskets were a joy to behold and Emily wondered where the proprietor of the pub had managed to get hold of such colourful plants. Flowers and plants were one of the worst shortages to bear during this long drawn out war. She had been told that in places such as Devon and Cornwall there was still an abundance of flowers. It was the transport that could not be spared to convey what the government felt forced to class as unnecessary luxuries.

Richard led the way, lowering his head because of the low beams of the ceiling, through a bar where several men were playing a game of darts. The next bar had five small tables each covered with a red check gingham table cloth.

A large, stout, rosy cheeked woman wearing a white overall and a white bonnet-shaped hat bade them welcome. She could, Emily thought, have come straight off the cover of Mrs Beeton's cookery book.

She led them to the only table that was not occupied and poured a glass of water for each of them. They were offered shepherd's pie, which smelt good and tasted really delicious and they followed it with a deep apple pie and custard.

Apologies were given that no cheese and biscuits were available. 'But me rock cakes would take some beating,' the landlady assured them, then, lowering her voice to a mere whisper she added, 'Them's got plenty of sultanas and currants in the mixture, compliments of the Americans who are stationed up the road. They scratch my back an' I scratch theirs, if yer see what I mean, me dears.'

So, Emily and Richard spent another half an hour over a pot of tea and some remarkably good warm rock cakes.

Richard couldn't take his eyes off Emily. He was fascinated by how the young girl he had known had grown into such a beautiful young lady, and he had been intrigued to learn that when this war finally came to an end her dearest wish was to live again in North Waltham.

They were the last people to leave the pub. They walked and then took the bus, doing the journey in reverse. Stretching out what little time they had left to be with each other, Richard suggested they went to the mess for a drink. It was the last thing that Emily wanted to do. If she were to come face to face with Clive Beaumont, especially if she were with Richard, she knew she would not know where to look. But Richard insisted.

Being a Sunday evening, the mess was quite busy. Emily began stacking the dirty glasses which had been left on one table and a steward, seeing her doing it, came quickly forward with a tray on which he placed the glasses and then using a spotless cloth he wiped the table clean for them. He also took an order from Richard for two brandies.

Emily looked around and breathed a sigh

of relief; there was no sign of Captain Beaumont.

When the drinks were placed in front of them, Richard was the first to raise his glass. 'Here's to our next meeting,' he said, sounding more jovial than he felt.

Emily knew that he was leaving at the crack of dawn for the airport and that she was not driving him.

The parting was painful, frustrating and annoying because Richard couldn't divulge his coming schedule even if he wanted to, and she had to keep reminding him that she was still in the ATS and that there wasn't a hell of a lot that she could do about it.

Richard remained unconvinced. 'Surely you could request some leave.'

'I have only just returned,' she said with a sorrowful laugh. 'Even you can't make the rules.'

'What about London? Even for a weekend? I'd love to take you to the theatre.' He felt he wanted to do so much for her. She deserved it. It wasn't just the driving; she had made him feel different. He couldn't explain it, only that he hadn't felt so good in a long time. And for once they weren't talking about work or the war. They were just two people who had known each other in the past, had come together and had spent a whole day in each other's company.

Except that they had no idea when they might meet again or even if they ever would, Emily thought dismally.

'It must be more than four years since you left home, Emily. Have you not met a young man that took your fancy?'

Emily looked puzzled. Why would he suddenly ask that?

'No one that I wanted a lasting association with,' she said simply. Then she dared to ask, 'Richard, are you married?'

He shrugged. 'No, I'm not, Emily. A few years back I nearly made it to the altar but...'

Emily wondered if she had upset him and she decided not to press him.

'Do you want to hear about it?' he volunteered.

'Only if you want to tell me.'

'She was a forceful young lady, very striking to look at. As a child her mother had pushed her into modelling. She grew fond of all the attention and I think I was too staid for her liking. But I think the finishing blow was when she firmly told me she didn't want to have any children.'

Richard remained quiet after that statement but Emily felt she had to ask.

'And did you decide that having children was important to you?'

'Yes, I did. I can't visualize a marriage without. What is the point? Unless one is unlucky and can't have children. I have always looked on a family as a great gift. Maybe because my own family has always been so loving.'

'You have two brothers, don't you?'

'Fancy you remembering that.' He smiled

'My parents used to talk about you three boys when we were small.'

'Yes, Frederick and Stanley started a business in Hong Kong with a settlement they got from our father, exporting metal goods and textiles. They were doing exceedingly well. I was with them six months before war broke out. My parents have been there several times but not in recent years.' He stopped talking and his face had turned a tinge of grey.

Emily knew that the colony had been occupied by the Japanese since December 1942. She couldn't bring herself to ask whether or not his brothers were safe.

Richard obviously did not want to talk about his brothers because he quickly turned the conversation around. 'You're very lucky, Emily, you've got great parents, and a great family life from what I've seen over the years.' He smiled warmly at her. 'I've always got on well with them, particularly your father because he always dealt with our horses.'

Emily was really pleased to hear him say that and she took a chance. 'If you get home soon, it would be nice if you called in to see my mum and dad, tell them we've met up.'

'I most certainly will,' he said, sounding as if he meant it. Then quickly he added, 'My own father and mother will be really interested when I tell them about you. But for now, Emily, we have to say goodbye. I've enjoyed your company immensely and I've had a great time today. You have been wonderful company.'

'I've enjoyed it too. Thank you, Richard.'

He walked with her to the main door and then only when they were alone and surrounded by darkness did he do what she had been longing for him to do. He took her in his arms and held her close and they stood still. Two people as one. Then he bent his head and covered her lips with his own. It was a soft, long, lingering kiss.

A kiss that she would remember for the rest of her life.

Then he took his arms from her and slowly

walked away. A few yards and he stopped and looked back, she was standing watching him go as he knew she would be.

He softly called, 'I am going to miss you.'

Silently, she told herself, and I'm going to miss him.

Very much.

# Sixteen

*1944*

For the first time since the declaration of war there were signs of weariness among the people. It was a miracle that they still had the energy and the resolution to keep going. The pilotless rocket planes had been the last straw that almost broke the camel's back.

During the past summer months these doodlebugs, as they had been named, had continually come crashing down on London streets in broad daylight. Sometimes there was not even time to sound a warning siren, so swift was their advance.

Now with only two months to go the

country was facing another bleak Christmas. This would be the sixth Christmas since Neville Chamberlain had declared that a state of war existed between England and Germany.

Tom's one great wish was that he might get home for Christmas. He had been very lucky of late, some of his friends down in the docks had told him if and when a cargo ship had got safely into harbour. Money hardly ever changed hands. It was more like bartering. It must have worked in the Stone Age and it had certainly worked for him since 1939. He had a stack of goods ready to take down to Hampshire and if he couldn't make it for Christmas he'd make sure he was there to see the New Year in.

Besides the goods, he also had a tidy sum of money stashed away. Being on munitions the money had been ten times what it would have been in peacetime, and it was Sam that had put him on the road to what he hoped would turn out to be a colossal success, not only for himself but for his beloved adopted family.

If things did go his way, and at this point he could see no reason why they shouldn't, then he was not only going to see to his own but to Agnes Brownlow, her two sons, and of course young Mary. Agnes had had a rough life at times but she was a truly kind-hearted and loving woman, and she had always held open house for John and himself. Tom never forgot a favour nor indeed a kindness. Agnes had never had much herself, but what she had she shared, and at a time when John and he had badly been in need of a helping hand she had been right there with Auntie Em and Uncle Sam. Well, he mused, get this bloody war over and I'll do me best to make it pay-back time.

He let his thoughts race back to the last time he had managed to be in North Waltham when a dance was being held. His funny, adorable Bella had been there and with her had been Mary Brownlow. God, that girl was growing into a real beauty! Coming up to sixteen years old she was, and he was sure that in another couple of years she would have the boys falling over them-selves to take her out.

You're sitting here dreaming about the past like a bloomin' old woman, he chided him-self; come on, you've got to get going to see Pete Kennedy. Now that was a problem that he had helped get sorted good an' proper and Pete, like the good bloke that he was, would never forget. He'd already put a few deals Tom's way and between them they'd slapped a few hands and let them know that even when doing dodgy deals there always has to be a code of honour!

Ron Leadbetter had been taught a lesson. Though strictly illegal, poor folk saw nothing wrong in taking a bet from the man in the street, but on the rare occasion that things went wrong the bookmaker should not abandon his street runner and the good folk that allowed him, for a paltry few shillings, to collect the bets from their doorsteps.

As for Jerry Faulkner, he had to learn that in the East End you treat women with respect and that nobody likes a liar. Especially a man who lays the blame on a young woman and on top of that lies to save his own skin.

Half an hour later Tom pushed open the front door and called loudly, 'It's only me.'

Pete Kennedy looked up the passageway then called back over his shoulder, 'Tess, gal, it's your saviour.' Pete was bare-chested, his braces hanging loosely from the waistband of his trousers, yet he still looked a fine figure of a man. Hand outstretched he laughingly said, 'Hi yer, Tom, an' how's the world treating you on this cold winter's morning?'

'Not so bad, mate, but not so good that I couldn't use a cuppa that's been well laced.'

Pete threw back his head and his laughter was enough to wake the dead. 'I take it yer've got the taste for our Irish Mist.'

'I have that right enough, Pete; it's a gift from the saints, so it is.'

'Come away in then an' take the weight off yer feet. Tess has just put the kettle on.'

Tom wasn't given a chance to sit down. Tessa came from the scullery into the living room and threw herself at Tom.

'Tom, my favourite bloke,' she exclaimed in a voice loud enough for the next-door neighbours to hear. 'Why 'ave yer not been around before this? It's a hell of a life you lead. You must've known that me and the girls wanted to thank you and do a bit of celebrating. Crikey, I still can't believe the way Jerry Faulkner changed his tune. That old magistrate wiped the floor with him, though for a moment or two when I saw him come into court with his arm in a sling I did feel just a mite bit sorry for him. Anyway, luv, sit yerself down. I've made the tea.'

Tessa poured tea into three mugs and Pete laced them. Silence prevailed while the two men appreciated their drink and Tessa drooled over hers until quite suddenly she put her mug down on to the table and started to giggle. It was only a matter of minutes until she was laughing uncontrollably.

Tom found it amusing but when he raised his eyebrows in question to Pete he was told, 'Leave her be, she'll come out of it soon. She often has these funny turns.'

Tessa's laughter did not fade away, but in between bouts she managed to say, 'Faulkner even said we could keep the goods which according to him we were supposed to have been going to wash.' More unruly chuckles, then, 'Like we were ever gonna give 'em back.' That last remark had them all in stitches.

When at last all was calm, Tom ventured to say, 'All's well that ends well, eh Tessa? Got off lightly on the other charge as well, didn't you?'

'Yeah, me mum reckons there was two reasons for that. One, a couple of the old men that were on the bench must 'ave been partial to horse racing, and secondly, they worked it out that if they fined me it was ten to one that Leadbetter would pay the fine. They were right an' all – public feeling was so much against him, he didn't get much choice. Cost him fifty quid,' Tessa managed to say before she went off into another fit of laughter.

'That geezer 'ad it coming to him. I reckon he'll take a bit more care of those that work for him in future otherwise he'll 'ave to start thinking about setting out a stand and only taking bets on the course, an' that'll cost him!' Pete told them firmly.

'I 'ope yer right.' Tom scowled. 'Otherwise a few of the bookies will be wanting a word with him.'

Tessa got up and walked unsteadily towards the scullery. 'I'm gonna make a fresh brew,' she slurred.

'How much Mist did you put in 'er tea?' Tom asked, smiling.

'Enough to keep 'er and me 'appy this afternoon cos I ain't on till ten tonight.' Pete winked at Tom before saying, 'I've got a list, and I'd like you to give it the once over. You, Tommy boy, can 'ave first crack at the whip 'cos it might be the last of anything good that we get our 'ands on this side of Christmas.'

Pete walked over to the dresser, opened a drawer and took out an envelope. 'Let me know soon as yer can. 'Fraid its got to be cash up front.' He faltered, then gave Tom a smile and said, 'Sorry, mate, I forgot Tommy

Yates don't do business any other way.'

'Dead right,' Tom grinned. 'Cash or the equivalent; that way it's smiles all round.'

'I'll drink to that,' Pete said, draining his mug.

Tom left the house feeling that his journey had been very fruitful. He had taken a quick look at the list that Pete had given him. There was now room for manoeuvre, he thought. One thing was certain. Lionel Trenfield would get what he had wished for this Christmas.

# Seventeen

Everything had gone wrong for Richard Trenfield.

However, that only applied to his personal life.

Business-wise he was aware of the fact that the war had done his career no harm. He was held in great esteem by his peers. Quite soon now the government's dream of a United Nations Organization would be realized. There were a great number of men, like himself who, though not having donned a uniform, had nevertheless played a part in helping England to fight the Germans.

Richard preferred to be a behind-the-scenes man. In spite of his obvious connections with the government, and the opportunities that could have afforded him, he had never felt the need to be a front man. He loved the excitement of what he did, and had no desire to draw attention to himself. In fact, it was often far more important to him to be seen but seldom heard.

At this point in time, it was his private life that he didn't know how to deal with.

He was on a plane coming back to London, having been away in Scotland for five weeks. So demanding had his work been that not once during the whole time had he been able to contact Emily. And he was still working when a stewardess asked him to fasten his safety belt as they were coming in to land.

Richard looked at her with a smile. 'What time is it?' he asked, stifling a yawn.

'Ten minutes past three, sir. Have you transport meeting you?'

'Yes I have, thank you,' he said firmly but then hesitated and said, 'At least, I hope so.'

'Let me know if you are stranded, sir, we

can always phone through.'

Richard thanked her again, wishing it could be that easy to contact Emily. He still couldn't come to terms with the effect that she had had on him. When he had first been informed that Emily Pearson was to be his driver he had thought it was just a rare coincidence that a young girl from the village where he lived had joined the ATS and was going to be driving the car that he would be using while he was in Colchester. When she had walked into the bar he hadn't been able to take his eyes off of her. He couldn't answer for her but on his part the thing that had sprung up between them, almost from the word go, had been extra-ordinary. Perhaps he was being absurdly romantic but before that week had been over he had known that she was the one he wanted to be married to. Oh, he had argued with himself that he was being stupid, that he was too old for her, but it had all been to no avail. Because of this wretched war he hadn't been able to tell her what work he was doing or even let her know of his where-abouts most of the time.

Had she felt the same way about him? Surely that was too much to hope for. He had known her as a cute little girl then as a leggy teenager, always with a gorgeous head of rich chestnut hair. Now she was a young lady, twenty-three or twenty-four years old, sophisticated and self reliant, who had left the safety of their village and found there was a big world out there. She was even serving in His Majesty's Armed Forces.

I don't want to make a fool of myself, he thought as he got his personal luggage down from the overhead lockers. If only there was a way I could find out whether she has any feelings for me.

He was getting more mournful by the minute.

Would she be going home for Christmas? Would he get a chance to see her before then? He gave a long drawn out sigh. Finding a partner, deciding you would like to live with them for the rest of your life, was almost like a lucky dip.

What does any of us know when we start up a relationship? Richard had been more than ready to walk up the aisle before Audrey had dropped the bombshell that she never wanted to have children. Once he had finished with university, and got his law degree, all he wanted was a rural family life, living in Hampshire, where everyone knew their neighbour and the simple pleasures of life were there for the taking. He wanted to have children, to bring them up as his parents brought up him and his brothers, but things never work out exactly as you expect them to. Maybe it was better like that, sometimes at least. His brothers' lives hadn't worked out the way they had expected either. He wondered sometimes if anyone's did.

He had made up his mind what he was going to do. From the airport he took a cab to his London apartment.

And the next morning he hired a car and was soon on his way to Colchester.

Maybe Emily wasn't still there, but anything was better than not knowing where she was and what her feelings towards him were, and no information would be available to him over the telephone.

Richard wasn't to know it, but Emily's feelings were running on a par with his. In fact, she had been having nightmares. Richard had been gone five weeks and never a word. Yet had he said he would be in touch with her?

No. What he had said was, 'I look forward to our next meeting'. That could be years from now. But if that was the case, why had he kissed her like that? It hadn't been a passionate kiss but it was no ordinary good-bye kiss between two friends either. She had to stop thinking about it. She was beginning to think it had never happened.

Richard stopped only the once on the journey to have a cup of coffee, go to the toilet and wash his hands; all the same it was dark when he arrived at the gatehouse of Colchester Barracks. He wasn't able to use his official identity cards that, if he were in London, would open almost every closed door. Here he was relying on being remembered. His request as to Corporal Pearson's whereabouts was met with greater keenness than he had a right to expect.

'Sir, it might make it easier for you if you wrote a little note,' the duty officer said shyly. 'I'll have it sent to the Corporal's quarters and if she wants to see you...' The poor woman was out of her depth. She knew that Mr Trenfield was a high-ranking businessman and had been here for a while on Government Licence. 'Maybe Corporal Pearson is not in barracks at all,' she finished lamely. Then quickly she offered, 'Would you like to wait in the mess?'

'Yes, I would, thank you, but I do need to park my car.'

'No problem, sir, our numbers are greatly depleted with so many personnel going on Christmas leave, so there is ample room in the car park. If you give me your keys I'll have it parked and you can pick your keys up here when you are ready to leave.'

It was less than twenty minutes when Emily came walking towards him.

'You're back,' she whispered.

He smiled as he nodded and then, lowering his head, he gently kissed her cheek. 'I missed you,' he said, pulling her close, and she could feel the warmth of his breath on her face as he kissed her again.

'I missed you too,' she said and somehow he knew that she meant it.

'Let's sit down,' he said, his voice a whole lot lighter than it had been earlier.

'Richard, I can't stay long, I'm on late duty this evening.' Suddenly she looked confused and her cheeks reddened.

He quickly asked, 'Is there something wrong?'

A smile quivered on her lips and her eyes were shining brightly as she blurted out, 'I called you Richard, straight off, just like that.'

'For which I am more than grateful. Emily, it will save us both a lot of time if we admit

211

that what we just said was true. We have missed each other and we are so glad that I have driven all the way from London on the off chance that I might get a glimpse of you. Is that true?'

'Absolutely,' she told him, grinning like a Cheshire cat.

'And now you are telling me that you have to be on duty tonight?'

'I have some good news as well as the bad news,' Emily said, still smiling.

'And that is?'

'I have seven days' leave as from midnight so I will be able to see you tomorrow.'

'Tomorrow,' he repeated, sounding horrified. 'If you are free as from midnight, I shall be waiting, underneath the lamp-light by the Barrack gates.'

Now there was no holding Emily's laughter. 'It's a wonder you didn't break into song since you said those most famous lines,' she managed to splutter.

'Tell me quickly, what plans have you made?' he asked urgently.

'Nothing definite; maybe do some Christmas shopping, stay one night in London and then go home. Mum will be upset that I haven't got leave over Christmas.'

'Right, pack your case before you go on

duty, then we can drive through the night, and you can stay at my flat, at least for one night, and we'll take it from there, shall we?'

So many questions were running through Emily's mind.

What flat? Where was it? And fancy him coming all this way to find her when there hadn't been even a postcard during the whole of the past five weeks. She wanted to take his face – the face that had haunted her dreams – between her hands and kiss it over and over again.

'How have you been?' he asked, breaking into her thoughts.

'Fine,' Emily said, smiling, 'much better now that I know you are safe. But my stretch of duty tonight is going to seem as if it is taking for ever. And, Richard – ' she reached for his hand – 'I do have to go. I was in the middle of pressing my uniform. I have so much to do, and I daren't be late.'

'I'll be waiting. I won't ask to come in past the gate, not in the middle of the night,' he laughed, 'but I'll be sitting in the car waiting to drive you for a change.'

'I can hardly believe it.' She smiled shyly then, and there was a moment's pause. 'I'm so happy to see you, Richard.'

So was he, happy to see her, and he felt

suddenly much younger. In so little time she had come to mean so much to him. He just could not put his feelings into words.

'I'm happy to see you too,' he said gently. 'I'll see you soon after midnight. We can make our plans then.'

Richard drove to the nearest hotel, parked his car, made a reservation for one for dinner, then went to the gentlemen's rest room. He washed his hands and face, took his shaving kit out of his overnight bag and had a quick shave. The dinner was pretty good and he lingered over coffee and just one small brandy. He felt that if he hung about much longer the staff might become suspicious, so he took himself off to the side street where he had left the car, unlocked it, started it up and drove back again to park a few yards up the road from the barracks, settled himself down in the driver's seat and waited.

The wait seemed interminable, and then at last he heard footsteps and she was standing there holding her suitcase. He got out of the car so quickly he almost fell over. He took the case from her, placed it on the back seat, straightened up and gave her a hug.

'I was so worried you might change your

mind and not want to come with me,' he confessed.

'I was worried too,' she admitted to him, 'but I'm all right now.'

He opened the door on the passenger side, handed her in and tucked a thick rug around her knees. It was a bright starry night but bitterly cold. For a moment Richard felt out of his depth. For the last five years his entire life had centred around his work except when he went home to Hampshire and spent time with his parents. He couldn't believe this was truly happening to him. He felt relaxed now as he looked down at the beautiful young girl who was tucked up in the front of his hired car. 'You look frozen,' he said with concern.

'The gatehouse is never warm at the best of times.' She shivered.

'What if I stop at the first all-night café, get you a hot drink? Maybe if we're lucky they might be serving hot soup.'

Emily nodded. She was so happy, smiling up at him, she could hardly concentrate on what he was saying.

As for Richard, all he wanted was to be with her. He thought it was a dream come true as he started the car and moved off. Presently he heard her softly sigh.

'Are you comfortable?' he queried.

'Yes, thank you, I'm just so contented. Nothing like this has ever happened to me before.'

Nor me, nor me, Richard was thinking, as he made himself keep his eyes on the road and concentrate on his driving.

An hour into the journey, Richard spied a café that had just one well-shaded lantern hanging high above the entrance. Having driven on to the forecourt, he held the door while Emily got out of the car and together they walked towards the café where Richard held back the dark grey blanket that had been hung as a black-out curtain and so enabled Emily to duck beneath it and enter into the warmth.

'Far from home, are yer?' the heavily-built proprietor, who looked to be all of seventy years old, asked as Richard approached the counter.

'Yes, we are, and this young lady is cold and hungry. Have you anything hot to offer her?' Richard suggested doubtfully.

The man took notice of the uniform Emily was wearing and smiled. 'Sit yerself down, lass, over there.' He pointed to a far corner of the room. 'There's an oil-heater on; don't give out much heat but yer can take yer shoes off and put yer feet on it if yer like.'

Emily took him at his word, and he turned to Richard. 'We've got plenty of tea and Camp coffee, and to eat there's Spam, corned beef, sausages and dried eggs, and of course the good old fall-back, dripping toast.'

Emily had heard every word and was grinning to herself. In all probability she was much more used to the kind of food that was being offered than ever Richard was.

He looked across at her, frowning hard. She helped him out. 'Please may I have a cup of tea and a sausage sandwich?'

'Of course yer can, me old darling,' the proprietor said kindly, reaching up to take an enormous tin tea-pot down from where it was standing on top of a brass urn.

Within a very short while Emily was sipping at a huge cup of tea that was at least five times stronger than she was used to. She didn't like it as strong as this but wild horses wouldn't have made her complain. And later, as she tried her best to eat her sausage sandwich with some degree of dignity, Richard asked, 'Have you any idea at all what went in to make those sausages?'

'None whatsoever,' she grinned as she tried to tear off a piece of the thick white bread with her front teeth. 'But I'll lay odds that I've eaten far, far worse since this war first started.'

Back in the car, Emily was fast asleep within minutes.

Only as Richard drove down through the Haymarket, into Trafalgar Square and along Shaftesbury Avenue where he turned into a row of prestigious houses, did she stir. Because of her war work she was very familiar with this area of London and she wasn't that surprised when Richard brought the car to a halt outside one of these great houses.

There was a grey light filling the sky as they walked towards the entrance. Richard was explaining that long before the war had started these houses had been made over into apartments. 'My apartment is on the very top floor,' he said gleefully and Emily pretended to look agitated.

'No need to look so worried, Emily my darling, there is a lift, and even if there were not I would have carried you up every step.'

'Easy to offer when you know you don't have to,' she scoffed but laughing all the same.

The workings of the lift were very slow but that suited Emily. She had butterflies in her stomach and she was glad that there hadn't been any residents about in the entrance hall as they had come in.

They stepped out on the fifth floor and Richard put his key into the lock of his solid-looking front door and stood back to allow her to enter his London home before him. The setting was spectacular, the furnishings exclusive, expensive but very comfortable-looking.

Emily was certainly impressed.

They each deposited the cases and boxes they had been carrying and they sat down. For a while they sat quietly, at ease with one another. They didn't need to say anything; they were both just enjoying a sense of fulfilment.

Presently Richard asked, 'Would you like to see your bedroom? And you can take a shower if you want, the water is always hot.'

'A shower would be great,' she murmured, as she stood in the entrance of the bedroom that Richard told her could be hers for as long as she felt the need of it. She was awe-struck. The room was enormous, with a very high ceiling, bare of anything that was not essential. No woman's touch had been given freedom in this bedroom.

Richard opened a wide cupboard, took out two hand towels and two bath sheets, and laid them on the bed. Then he took down a coat-hanger from which was hanging a thick fluffy towelling robe.

'The bathroom is the second on the left and the shower room is opposite on the right. Just shout if you need any thing.' Richard turned to go, then half turned back. 'You will probably want to have a good sleep before we decide if we are going out anywhere today. Don't bother about the time, sleep as late as you like. Isn't it a marvellous thing to be able to say – time is our own?'

She took a shower, using lovely-smelling fragrances that she hadn't seen for years, and wondering how Richard had such a good supply of expensive soaps in both his bathroom and the shower room. Her hair felt the cleanest and looked the most shiny that it had been for ages and she was sorry that it wasn't long enough to hang down over her shoulders as it used to before army regulations had been forced on to her.

She came out wrapped in the white robe, her bare feet padding on his lovely carpets and when Richard saw her he gasped. She might have grown some, but at that moment she looked just like the small girl that he used to meet in the lanes when she and her sister Arabella were walking their dog or coming home from school.

A sense of panic ran through him. Was he doing the wrong thing? He couldn't help himself, and neither apparently could she.

It was Emily that crossed the space that was between them. She put her arms around his neck, and she kissed him. Then he sat down with her on his lap and he kissed her. They sat like that for a long time, holding on tightly to each other.

'I shouldn't have brought you here,' he whispered finally, 'but I do love you so much, Emily.'

'I love you too, Richard,' she said softly. It wasn't just desire that ran between them. It was as if they had known each other all of their lives; he had been there and so had she yet they had never come together. Now they had found each other there could be no going back. From this moment in time they were as one.

She was the first to move. She stood up and the towelling robe fell open and he gently slipped it off her shoulders, and she was standing naked before him. A moment later he picked her up and carried her into his bedroom. He laid her on the bed and she watched as he took his clothes off.

Slowly and gently his hands roamed all over her, and as their lips met, she moaned.

Richard wanted to tell himself to stop, that this was wrong. But he knew in his heart of hearts it was not.

Emily was thrilled to be giving herself to the man whom she felt so strongly about, who had known her for years. Well, now she had and he was claiming her and everything seemed so right. Her own feelings told her that she loved every part of this man and, not only that, she absolutely adored him.

He looked down at her, her thick hair lying tousled and silky on his pillow; she reached up and put her arms around his neck, pulled his head down and they slowly kissed each other.

It was quite some time later, as they lay contented side by side, that he said, 'Emily, there is something that I have to tell you.'

He sounded so serious that for a moment she felt fearful.

Raising herself up by resting on her elbows she looked into his eyes.

'I'm listening,' she said.

Richard's voice was very serious as he said, 'Emily, you have to find the time to marry me.'

If he had said she had to walk on the moon she couldn't have been more surprised.

'And where did that come from?' she at last managed to ask.

'Certainly not out of the blue,' he loudly declared. 'In ordinary times of peace I wouldn't have dreamed of making love to you before you had become my wife. But these are uncertain times, and we've both learnt to take happiness when and if it comes along. The chance can so often be lost. Having found you, I quickly realized that I loved you from the start and now, having made love to you, I demand that you make an honest man of me. If you were to say no I should have to go and live in foreign parts because I should never again be able to hold my head up high.'

'You're mad!'

'Probably, yes. You think I am too old for you, is that it?'

'Well, yes, you probably are,' she said, trying hard to sound serious. 'But then again the government will pay me to look after you in your old age and I can always hire a bath chair in which to wheel you to the post office to enable you to draw your old age pension.'

She never did get to hear his answer to that

because he had pulled her down flat again, and was preparing to lie on top of her once more and prove again that he wasn't that old.

# Eighteen

To Emily, these last few hours spent with Richard in his apartment had been unbelievable. She felt she had never been happier in her life. There was no doubt in her mind: she was in love with Richard, and he with her. To add to her joy the darling man had told her, twice in the last half hour, *our dream is only just beginning.*

All she wanted now was to stay in these beautiful rooms, be alone with him, so they could talk and touch each other, just so that she could really and truly convince herself that the happenings of the last few hours had not been a figment of her imagination.

Richard had other ideas, as he lay on his side, looking at her, slowly tracing a finger down the curves of her body. What they had shared so far had served to reassure him that his feelings had been absolutely right. At least for now they were shut away from everyone and everything; the war for them had been put on hold. He looked into Emily's eyes; she looked happy and peaceful. They knew they loved each other.

But for now he had to coax her to get dressed and come to the shops with him.

'Emily, will you please get dressed?' he asked for the second time.

'Richard, why do we have to go anywhere or do anything? Why don't we just stay as we are, enjoy each other's company while we can?'

'Because, my darling, I have a most important purchase to make. I shall dress and then I have a couple of telephone calls to make.' He had to tear himself away from her arms and later he found she was still lingering in the shower room.

He knocked on the door and, when she called out, 'I won't be long,' he said softly, 'I'm missing you.'

Emily opened the door a crack. 'And I'm missing you. Do you want to come in?' she whispered.

'You have the advantage of me. You're a tease, standing behind the door when I know you're naked, while I'm ready to go. I've made my calls and our first appointment is in forty minutes; the taxi will be here in ten.'

'Richard, you can't do that to me; I can't be ready in ten minutes.'

'Then I shall have to go without you.'

They were like a couple of kids goading each other.

When the intercom buzzer sounded and a voice said, 'Mr Trenfield, your taxi is here,' they held hands and ran to the lift laughing and sounding happy, though Emily was feeling a little agitated. Richard, as always, looked as if he'd just come out of a bandbox, whereas all she had to wear was her ATS uniform. She had her greatcoat over her arm but it was so heavy and bulky she wished she had a few more clothing coupons; if she toured enough shops while she was in the West End of London she just might come across one that had a decent raincoat or, even better, a decent winter coat left in stock. Apart from the odd jumper or blouse, she hadn't been able to buy many decent clothes since the start of the war and there were times when she tired of her uniform.

The taxi drew up at the far end of Hatton Garden and Emily felt a moment of panic. Why had Richard brought her here? Was she getting in too deep? Again, from her wartime experiences, she had gained the knowledge that Hatton Garden was the centre of the diamond trade. As the driver was holding the cab door open for her to step down and Richard was taking money from his wallet, the door to the premises was opened and an elderly gentleman wearing a black long-tailed coat and pin-striped trousers came out and stood at the top of the stone steps leading to the door. It was obvious that Richard was expected.

Most of London, including a great number of business premises, had suffered from the air raids and certainly no plate glass windows remained intact. Most had been shattered, and were now boarded up. Hatton Garden dated back to well before Dickens' time, or at least it seemed so to Emily. How well she remembered the pictures on the walls of their school library, bow-fronted shop windows with small circular panes of thick glass. This moneyed area was in a class of its own.

'Welcome, Mr Richard.' The gentleman had his hand outstretched.

'How d'you do, Mr Austin? It was good of you to see us on such short notice,' Richard said smiling, as he brought Emily forward

227

saying, 'This is my fiancée, Emily Pearson. Emily, this is Mr Austin, a great friend of my parents.'

Mr Austin bowed his head, then taking Emily's hand he smiled, and said, 'A great pleasure to meet you, Miss Pearson.'

'How d'you do, Mr Austin?' Emily murmured, as she and Richard were ushered toward a winding staircase. Dangerous, Emily was thinking as she climbed, thankful, for once, that she was not wearing high-heeled shoes.

'I have suggested a collection of rings to be laid out in the velvet room.' Mr Austin spoke directly to Richard as they reached the safety of a landing. 'I am handing you over to Mr Jeremy.' Then lowering his voice he added, 'He is a good number of years younger than myself, so he'll be better able to offer advice on your choice. Do come and take a drink with me before you leave.' He patted Richard's arm, bowed again to Emily and with great dignity he left them.

Emily was by no means stupid. She had worked out for herself that Richard wanted to purchase a ring for her. But it was almost unreal. It was as if she was on the outside looking in at some play or another. Things were moving so fast. It couldn't be happening, not for real it couldn't.

Inside the room they went through all the rigmarole of introductions once again until at last *young* Mr Jeremy – who to Emily's way of thinking was sixty years old if he were a day! – pointed to where two high-backed chairs had been placed facing a long glass-topped table upon which a length of black velvet had been laid out.

Richard nodded for Emily to sit down and he took the other chair. Under the guise of making herself comfortable, she whispered, 'You, Mr Richard, are going to pay dearly for this.'

Richard deliberately made out that he had misunderstood her. 'Darling Emily, no expense is to be spared; my wife shall have the ring of her choice.' However, he was unable to completely hide his grin.

Mr Jeremy had disappeared into what seemed to be a walk-in vault.

Emily glared at Richard. 'You know darn well I was not alluding to the cost of any ring. You are a deceitful man. You got me here under false pretences.'

'Whoa! Are we having our first quarrel? Because if we are I would so much rather you waited until we get home, and then the making up could be oh so wonderful.' Still wearing a grin, but not looking anywhere near so self-assured, he reached out and took her hand into his and it was that moment that Mr Jeremy came out of the vault carrying four flat black boxes, each with a golden clasp.

He seated himself behind the counter, laid all four boxes out in a row and raised each lid. Not a word was spoken. A pin, if dropped, would have been heard.

Emily just stared, thinking of only one word: dazzling!

She was saying over and over to herself, I have to be dreaming. I shall wake up soon. Then the tears will flow.

It couldn't be a dream. Richard was holding her by the elbow and urging her to lean forward to enable her to take a closer look.

'Darling, there is no hurry. Just take your time, try on as many rings as you like. I'll help if you like. Would you like diamonds or do you prefer some colour in the stones, say a ruby or a sapphire?'

Emily could not let him go on. Whether it was good manners or not she had to do what her heart was telling her to. She held her head high and looked directly at Mr Jeremy. 'Sir, would you mind if Mr Richard and I leave the room for a few minutes? There is just a small matter that I need to discuss with him.' She was shaking like a leaf but also her tummy was rumbling with hysterical laughter. And God knows what might happen if she let it all out.

She had been going to suggest that Mr Jeremy leave the room and then the thought had come to her that he might think she was after putting a ring or two into one of her many pockets. This whole thing was farcical. It was unbelievable. This could not be happening to her.

The colour had drained from Richard's face. Now he was worried that his surprise might have back-fired, and he wouldn't have wanted to upset Emily for the world.

Mr Jeremy held the door open for them and pointed to a door on the opposite side of the landing. 'It is only a store-cupboard but there is just enough room for the pair of you to turn round in. Take your time,' he said to Richard, 'there is no hurry.'

Squashed up together, Richard's eyes were full of love as he gently took her into his arms. 'I take it I have upset you by springing my surprise on you. Emily, I did it from the best of intentions. I took advantage of you by making love to you when you were feeling very vulnerable. We met, and I think we both of us fell in love. Then I had to leave you, I was unable to contact you, and when I did reappear we seemed to fall into each other's arms. And after I had made love to you I felt I had to...' He stopped; floundering. 'No, no, those are not the right words; there was no *had to*, I needed to prove to you that my intentions were honourable, that I wasn't using you, and now...'

'Richard, will you please listen to me for one moment?' she implored. 'You have nothing to blame yourself for, because I don't think that what we did was in any way wrong. We are adults and it was a mutual decision.'

'Then tell me what is so important that we had to break off from choosing an engagement ring for you and end up in a store cupboard?'

Now it was Emily who was embarrassed. She knew she had to answer but the words would come hard. It would immediately show the great difference in their way of life.

'Richard, don't be cross, but you sat there telling me to choose whether I wanted diamonds, rubies or whatever, and I ... I have no idea what those rings cost. They were all of them so beautiful, but how was I to know how much you wanted to spend?'

'Oh, good Lord above!' The sigh that Richard gave came from deep within his heart and as Emily watched she saw his eyes brim with tears. 'What a blasted fool I've been.' He slapped the palm of his hand against his forehead and was swearing beneath his breath. 'How in God's name could I have been so thoughtless? I could have brought you a ring and told you some cock and bull story about it having belonged to my grandmother.'

He gently held her to him. 'Would you like to go back and choose a ring now?'

'No, may we leave it for now, and when you feel like it, please, will you choose one? And if you like it, then so will I.'

'Very well, my darling, if that is the way that you want it, that is how it shall be. Just one thing, will you come back with me now and let Mr Jeremy try a ring card on your finger to make sure that I get the right size?'

Emily agreed to that and as they came out of the cupboard they stood dusting themselves down and simultaneously they saw the funny side of the situation. It was a hard job for each of them to smother their chuckles before they went back to face Mr Jeremy.

'I want you to listen to one more request,' Richard warned, putting his arm out to stop her from moving. 'When we leave here we are going to do some real shopping. I cannot bear to see you having to wear your uniform at all times, especially that great heavy coat.'

'Oh, Richard, you are a darling, and I love you for being so thoughtful, but the reason I haven't got any winter clothes, other than issue, is because I don't have any clothing coupons left, or only one or two, which certainly wouldn't get me a coat.'

'For once, Emily, just once, will you let me come with you; you may choose whatever you need and leave the gory details to me. Please, will you do that?'

'Yes, I will, and thank you.'

'Right, I'm going to hold you to that. I don't want you mentioning or worrying about coupons or money. We'll just see if together we can find a London store that still has a few winter coats for sale.'

They spent the rest of the morning going from one department store to another without much luck. The odd few coats that they did find were mostly a drab grey or brown and looked as if they had been made from an old army blanket, which indeed they might well have been.

In Regent Street they stopped to have a light lunch and it was here that Richard got into conversation with the manager of the catering section.

He came back to the table where Emily was still drinking her coffee, his face wreathed in smiles.

'It is not what you know but whom you know, more often than not in this life,' he assured her. Then added, 'Even more so during wartime.'

Much later, full after a huge lunch which included many rationed items, and laden down with parcels, Richard suggested they take food home with them rather than come out again to eat this evening. Emily was all for that, and even more so when Richard held open the door to the shop and the smell of so much gorgeous food filled her nostrils. The proprietor, dressed from head to toe in pure white, came striding across the shop floor to enthusiastically greet Richard. She couldn't help but wonder how come Richard knew all the right people and all the right places to go to.

In some ways she found herself comparing Richard with Tom. That sounded ridiculous even to herself. Even so, they both seemed to have acquired a knack of always being in the right place at the right time, *and* of knowing all the right people.

By eleven o'clock that night, they were both in the one bed, curled up in each other's arms. Emily was tired but she was having a problem sorting out the events of the day in her head so could not sleep. Richard had made love to her, proposed to her, tried to buy her an engagement ring, had bought her an entirely new winter outfit and shown her that good food was still available if you knew where to look, even though England was still fighting a war against the Germans. And all within the space of twenty-four hours.

Richard broke into her thoughts. 'If I let myself fall asleep, will you promise to still be here when I wake up?' he said, as he lay next to her, cuddled up against her back, with his arms around her holding her close to him.

'I'm not going anywhere. In fact, I'm afraid to go to sleep in case I wake up to find out today was all a dream,' she told him firmly.

'Darling, it was no dream. Today has been the beginning of our life together and the sooner I can make an honest woman out of you the safer I shall feel.'

'What? You still want to marry me? Even after today?' she exclaimed, but she laughed as she said it.

'Emily, will you believe me when I tell you

that as soon as possible we shall be going to Hampshire together, and I shall formally ask your father's permission to have you for my wife. Is that going to be all right by you?'

'Richard, that sounds so final, and yet I still can't quite believe it. Oh, and another thing, what about your parents?'

'What about them? I can tell you this much, they have almost given up on me making a good marriage. You, they will consider to be manna from heaven, and they will love you as much as I do. Now I think it is about time you closed your eyes and got some sleep.'

'Is that an order?' she asked sleepily.

'Yes,' he whispered gently. And minutes later, when he raised his head and looked at her, she was sound sleep; he gently pulled the eiderdown further up the bed and tucked it around her.

# Nineteen

Neither Tom nor Emily made it home for Christmas. Only cards had been exchanged, for by mutual agreement all gifts had been put on hold until New Year's Eve.

Today was the thirtieth of December, and the Pearsons' cottage was a very happy place to be. Emily was sitting on the floor, her legs stretched out in front of her, her back resting against her mother's knees.

Emma thought she would burst with happiness as she gently stroked her daughter's silky hair, but at the same time she was totally confused by everything that she had been told.

Bella also was sitting on the floor. She was stacking gift-wrapped parcels beneath the bay window in readiness for the great share-out which was to take place tomorrow. Every now and again Bella lifted her head and smiled at her sister. Her heart swelled with joy as she stared at the diamond ring that was on the third finger of Emily's left hand.

Sam had Tom for company. The very fact that Richard Trenfield had driven their Emily down from London yesterday, had come into the house on arrival but had only stayed long enough to ask his permission to marry his daughter, had shaken Sam to the very roots.

They had shaken hands, Sam had slapped Richard on the back, and Richard had assured him they would celebrate on New Year's Eve. He wanted to get home and give his own parents the good news before they heard it from anyone else.

'Shall we walk up to the Fox?' Sam now gingerly suggested to Tom.

'Not the best of ideas,' Tom said, looking out of the window. 'Good job we all decided to travel yesterday; the roads today would be nigh on impossible.'

'Yeah, that was some snowfall last night, and the fact that everywhere is frozen solid this morning hasn't helped,' Sam said, smiling thoughtfully.

'Looks great, though,' Bella said and laughed. 'Like a winter wonderland.'

'You think so, do you?' Tom teased. 'Well, put yer boots on and find a woolly hat and you can come outside with me to fetch in a stack of logs. Don't want Mum venturing out there.' Then turning to Sam, he said, 'You get the glasses and I'll go upstairs and bring down a bottle or two. We don't have to wait until tomorrow to toast the happy couple; we'll have a private celebration all of our own.'

And they did.

It was still wartime but no stranger passing through the village of North Waltham would have known. New Year's Eve of 1944 was a day that would be remembered by the locals for many a long day.

Richard had a word with some of the top brass who were occupying the Big House. An instant decision had been made. It was appropriate that the large dining room should be thrown open for an impromptu celebration not only to see the New Year in but also to mark the fact that Mr Trenfield's son had become engaged to a local young lady. 'Open House' was to be the order of the day.

There was still an hour to go before the New Year would be rung in.

Richard grabbed hold of Emily as she walked by and practically pushed her out of the room and into the vast hall. 'Wow, what a do!' he laughed. 'It almost feels as if we have the League of Nations here with us tonight,' he said, as he drew her tenderly into his arms. 'Are you happy, Emily?'

'Delirious would be a better word and so proud. Your mother and father have been absolutely wonderful. There was no need for them to venture out and come to our house this morning.'

'Emily, they came because they wanted to. I told you they would be overjoyed and now you know I was speaking the truth. They both love you, and already I'm sure my mother is anticipating the pleasure of having grandchildren.'

Emily felt her cheeks flush, a fact that made Richard smile as he whispered, 'More than half the residents of this village have kissed you today but you have been neglecting me. Promise you'll make it up to me later.'

'Starting right now,' she eagerly agreed, holding her face up while Richard took her at her word.

Bella had been dancing with both the Americans and the Canadians when Tom found her sitting one dance out. 'The band is still playing,' Tom said. 'Why are you not dancing?'

'Bit breathless, some of the Yanks are pretty exhausting,' she said with a smile.

Tom held out his hand, pulling her to her feet, and said, 'Let's go and get a plate of food and a drink and find somewhere quiet, shall we?'

'All right,' she agreed quickly. 'It will be nice to escape the crowds for a little while. It has been one heck of a day. Beyond belief really, but then news travels fast in a village as small as this and Emily has always had loads of friends.'

They had the choice of so much food, because everyone had thought it was such a good idea to see the New Year in all together, and what the locals couldn't supply in the way of food the military had. Tom carried their plates and Bella followed him to a wide window seat where they settled quite cosily. Moving the heavily lined tapestry curtains to one side Bella sat gazing out at a white world that now, with the light fading, was tinged with blue. Every tree looked as if it had been personally decked out for New Year, with every leaf and branch heavy with the glistening snow.

They ate in a comfortable silence until

their plates had been cleared and Tom handed Bella a glass of wine and for himself he raised a brandy goblet to his lips.

'Bella, I would like you to know that I am very envious of Richard.'

Tom's words were said so forthrightly that Bella was really hurt. She mentally shook herself and, putting on as blank a stare as she could manage, she murmured, 'Don't suppose you're the only one. I should think that more than half the men in this room have been in love with our Emily at one time or another.'

'*What!*' The one word shot from Tom like an explosion.

Bella drew herself back from him. His eyes were blazing, but why she couldn't fathom. Did he think he was the only one that was allowed to love Emily?

'Bella,' he roared, 'are you blind? Whatever gave you the idea that I was in love with Emily. Yes, I do love her to bits, there isn't anything in this world that I wouldn't do for her, but I am not *in* love with her.'

'Then why the hell did you say you envied Richard?' Bella cried out spitefully.

Tom sighed heavily and clenched his fists. 'Because of you, yer dumb ha'porth, but he had the guts to tell Emily how he felt and to ask her to marry him.'

Now Bella's thoughts *were* in a muddle and she was close to tears. I won't let him see me cry, she vowed, but there was no need for him to shout at me like that and to call me dumb.

Without warning, Tom's whole attitude changed, and he reached out and gently drew Bella close. With his arms loosely wrapped around her he searched for the right words to say. 'Bella, my darling, you are the girl that I have loved and adored since I was ten years old. It has taken me a heck of a long time to reach this point but I think that today is the day when I should tell you just how much you mean to me.'

Bella didn't dare to move; she so very much wanted to believe that every word Tom had just said was true. In any case, he was still holding her in his arms and at this moment it was a lot more than she had ever dared to hope for.

'I have always been afraid that you looked upon me just as a brother and nothing more,' he said, sheepishly, 'and there seemed to be so many good reasons why I couldn't openly tell you that I loved you and wanted you all to myself.'

'Oh, Tom, you great nut! Remember when

you and John absconded from the institution and we couldn't find you, didn't know where you were or how you were living? I wanted to die – ask Mum – I didn't eat properly, wouldn't get out of bed, I cried all the time. I thought I was never going to see you ever again. What does that tell you? And when you did come back you never seemed to have any time for me.'

Tom smiled, but it was a sweet sad smile.

'You were a kid. You're not trying to tell me that those feelings have lasted all this time.'

'I was only one year younger than you and you have just told me that you have loved and adored me since you were ten. Why should it be any different for me?'

Tom sighed, but it was a soft sigh of pure regret as he folded her into his arms, letting her head lie against his broad chest. He lowered his head and kissed her long thick curly hair, pleased that the Land Army regulations had never insisted that female workers should have their hair cut short.

For a long while neither of them moved, each content with the fact that they had eventually come to know the feelings that they had for each other.

'Tom, why did you never let me know how you felt about me?' Bella at last found the courage to ask.

'Oh, I don't know.' He turned her a little, but still keeping her in his arms he was now able to see her sweet face. 'It never seemed to be the right time.' But he wasn't convincing.

'Please, Tom, I need to know.'

'You want the true reason? I was afraid. I know it sounds daft but Mum, Dad, Emily and you had taken John and me into your home, loved us, made us part of the family. It seemed to me that I would be taking too many liberties, robbing them of their youngest daughter to worm my way deeper into their family. Then came the war. You were still so young, you'd never been anywhere, not seen anything of life except the peace and quiet of Hampshire. To top everything else, the Canadians, Americans, all sorts were living and working in this small village. I pondered long and hard, came up with the idea it wouldn't be fair on you. Thought it only fair to step back, stay in the background, let you see a bit of life, find out if you fancied anyone else. But now, I suppose I should thank Richard and Emily for making me see sense. Because – ' he paused and sat up straight – 'if you had come to me and told me you were going to marry someone else I think I should have been driven to murdering him.'

'You great fool, Tom,' Bella said, sounding sad. 'Are you now saying you want to marry me?'

'It looks that way, doesn't it? That's if you'll have me,' he said with all sincerity.

'Oh, Tom, the answer is yes, yes. But only if you are willing to do one thing for me.'

'And that is...?' he asked cautiously.

'You have to get down on one knee and ask me properly.'

'No sooner said than done, my fair lady.' True to those words he hitched the legs of his trousers up a little and knelt on one knee. Taking hold of her left hand he said, 'Arabella Pearson, please will you marry me, because my dearest wish is to have you for my wife.'

Tears welled up in Bella's eyes as she now clung to Tom. He was the boy she had fallen in love with when she was still at school. How often she'd thought of him as Jack-the-lad, living in London with the choice of all sorts of women, and now here he was telling her that it was her that he wanted as his wife. Suddenly she was terrified – how near she had come to losing him. It was Richard she had to thank, for if he hadn't brought Emily home with a ring on her finger, telling the whole world that no matter what, he was going to marry the girl he had fallen in love with, would Tom have declared his love for her?

Tom's thoughts were running along the same lines. Because of his own stupidity he had almost lost Bella.

'When are we going to tell Mum and Dad?' Bella asked, shyly.

'Kiss me first an' then I'll tell you,' Tom said, in his own cocky way.

The next few minutes were like a dream, a dream that she never wanted to end.

Finally Tom took his lips away from hers and she was left breathless, but still held nestling in his arms.

'To be fair to Emily and Richard, I think we should keep our news until after midnight. This is their day and our news won't hurt for keeping back for a few hours. What do you think, Bella?'

Bella looked straight into his eyes. 'Tom Yates, I know you do your damnedest to let people think otherwise, but I know that you are a decent man, kind and fair. I know for a fact that if you can't do someone a good turn you would always hesitate before you'd do them a bad one. Yes, my darling Tom, I am quite willing to wait and tell Mum and Dad that you have asked me to marry you on the first day of the New Year.'

'I'm gonna tell them that I finally got smart and realized what a good catch you are.' Tom was still trying to joke, but his words were said in a choked voice.

For the next three hours, it was partying all the way. Bella and Tom were never off the dance floor and Emily and Richard were making themselves good runners up.

Sam Pearson looked knowingly at his wife several times as the minutes ticked by.

Then, with only minutes to go, Lionel Trenfield asked the drummer of the band to beat out a drum-roll. It took a few minutes for silence to fall in that great hall and most people drew their memories of the past year close to them. Few had really happy memories, and so many young men here this evening were from far away countries and were thinking longingly of home.

A sad reminder that the war had not ended was the fact that for the sixth year running the church bells would not be rung. No fireworks could be set off and no lights could be shown. The New Year was heralded in with good wishes, hugs and kisses mingled with a whole lot of tears.

★ ★ ★

Emily and Richard said a lingering goodbye. He was staying in the bungalow with his parents and he was going to see them safely home.

Sam, Emma and Tom produced torches, as did Agnes, Sid and Lenny. Emily, Bella and Mary tucked their long skirts up and the nine of them began to slowly walk home.

It was the Brownlows' house they came to first, where the parting was emotional with seventeen-year-old Mary declaring she had never thought such a night would have been possible, and Agnes saying she would call round some time later in the day.

Emma's reply to her dear friend was, 'Please, make it late afternoon. God knows what time any of us will get out of our beds.'

Hardly had the Pearson clan set foot inside the house, than Tom had cornered Sam and for the second day running Sam was listening to a young man asking him for his permission to marry his daughter.

This time Emma simply burst into tears. Floods of them were running down her cheeks and everyone laughed as she emphatically stated that she had never felt so happy before in her whole life.

★ ★ ★

As the early days of 1945 slipped by, the end of the war seemed to be in sight.

The inhabitants of southern England, and of London in particular, especially prayed this might be so, because the last stand from Germany was rockets. The very threat of these awful machines bringing instant death served only to revive fears of the worst horrors of the Blitz.

Their prayers were answered.

Hitler had killed himself. Then, on May the seventh, Germany signed a declaration of unconditional surrender.

Next day, May the eighth, 1945, Winston Churchill broadcast an announcement. The war against Germany was finally over.

As news of the German surrender flashed up and down the country, people took to the streets.

London was alive once more. In Piccadilly, all along the Strand, down the Haymarket and into Trafalgar Square, every solitary thing ground to a halt. City life had become a carnival and Emily watched it all with Richard's arms closely enfolding her as they stood watching the crowds from the high balcony of Richard's apartment. After five and a half years of total war, nobody seemed quite sure exactly when it was all over. And at that point in time it was certain that nobody really cared.

The war was over.

# Twenty

Emma Pearson was so happy, thrilled to bits that everything in her life was going so well, yet at times that very fact frightened her to death. Two weddings were coming up, both of her girls with partners that would love and take care of them, on that score she had no misgivings. The bonus was that neither couple wanted to up and move away from this village where they had been born. Unbelievable almost, that she and Sam would be able to see their girls pretty often even after they were married. The way things had turned out it was certainly true to say that they would be gaining two sons rather than losing two daughters. She shook her head in doubt, even talking to herself; it all sounded too good to be true.

After six years of war, was the world now coming back to some form of normality? To a certain degree, yes. Yet even with all the rejoicing and street parties, that were so well deserved by the British people who had suffered so much, there were many who could only stand by and watch with aching hearts. So many young sons, brothers and husbands would never be coming home. Rationing of all essential foods still continued, and housing all over England was in short supply. The final destruction of Germany was completed and people felt some compassion for the German people who had been led by Hitler and his Nazism, until news came over the wireless that the American troops had overrun the East German Buchenwald concentration camp. The liberators found twenty-one thousand starving survivors and thousands upon thousands of corpses.

A week later Emily and Bella had gone into Basingstoke to see the film *National Velvet*. When they returned home early both Emma and Sam had needed no telling that something was radically wrong. The look on their daughters' young faces was something that Emma felt she would be haunted by for the rest of her life. The Pathe newsreel had shown that British troops were discovering dozens of such camps throughout Germany and Eastern Europe, including Belsen and Auschwitz. Emma silently prayed for the troops who were there, in those hellish places where thousands of Jewish people had been gassed every day for months on end. In every camp, the Germans had taken care to destroy as much evidence as they could, but the piles of human ash and thousands of corpses were evidence of mass human extermination.

The end of the War in Europe was celebrated around the world, and nobody would deny the crowds that congregated in Trafalgar Square, London, on VE Day their high spirits. During the months leading up to the first peacetime Christmas, life had to some extent resumed an air of normality. At least it had in the village of North Waltham, Emma Pearson would repeatedly tell herself.

Richard Trenfield had his and the lives of his loved ones organized down to the last detail. It had taken six months to oversee the departure of the troops from the Big House and the surrounding grounds. It had been his parents' own decision to continue to live in the cottage. However, by the Christmas of 1945 Richard had insisted that his parents temporarily move back into a small part of the Big House while modern plumbing and other renovations were carried out on the much smaller property.

During that period of time Richard remained in London from Monday to Friday, coming home every weekend. He intended to keep his London apartment for the foreseeable future because it would be nigh on impossible for him to cut all business ties with the City and live solely in North Waltham, much as he would have liked to. That would have to come later.

With their wedding date provisionally set for the autumn of 1946, Emily had never for a moment imagined that the Big House would become their family home. Richard and his wonderful parents had put forward such persuasive arguments, the main one being that their two eldest sons had been killed in the battle for Singapore and that the house would die if it were not used as a family home. Very reluctantly, Emily had in the end given in to their gentle persuasion. It was the fact that if and when she and Richard did take up residence she might be thought of as being the lady of the manor and that very thought petrified her.

So many discussions! So much planning! There were times when Emily wondered just what had she let herself in for. It would take months, perhaps even years, before all the work and alterations that Richard had in mind could be completed on this vast property. With great persistence, and a lot of jovial doggedness, he finally had her believing that the end would justify the means.

Emma shook her head in doubt but a wide grin was spreading on her face as she imagined herself and Sam going through that massive front door one Sunday afternoon in the future to take tea with her Emily and Richard. What if it came about that in the near future they would be able to take some small toys and a few sweets for their grandchildren? She opened her mouth and let out a bellow of a laugh, at the same time chiding herself to show a bit of restraint because that really was putting the cart before the horse.

Emma was still laughing as she went out into the back garden. She had a large enamel bowl perched on one hip and already her eyes were scanning the lines of vegetables that were growing in the rich dark earth. Emily had written that she was to be given her final demob papers this week and hopefully she would be home for the weekend. Bella and Tom would definitely be home by then so she would need plenty of vegetables and a load of potatoes if she were going to put on a proper roast Sunday lunch for all of them.

Bella had already been demobilized from the Women's Land Army but for a while yet she was going to continue to work for Jack and Joyce Briggs up at Corner Farm. Meanwhile Jack had agreed that Bella could take two weeks' paid holiday. Tom had grabbed at the chance to take Bella to London to meet Daisy and Donald Gaskin and their vast family. Bella insisted that she had previously met Daisy and Donald when her parents had taken her to London, but she did agree that it had been a very long time ago and she probably wouldn't recognize either of them.

Emma had been apprehensive when Tom first talked about introducing Emily to the Gaskins, but for all Emily's upper crust way of speaking and her gentle manner the whole family had taken to her. Would it be the same for their Bella? Oh, with all her heart Emma prayed that it would be so, but she had her doubts. Bella was such a home bird; rarely had she ever travelled further afield than her Hampshire domain. London and the whole of the Gaskin tribe? The very thought would be enough to scare the living daylights out of poor Bella!

No one need have troubled themselves. According to Bella's first letter the whole Gaskin clan had taken to Bella like a duck to water, and she to them by all accounts.

At the back end of June, only weeks after the war had ended, Tom had attended an auction, which was being held in London. First, Tom had dug deeply and had come up with several reasons why he should make a bid, reasons that to him made a whole lot of sense.

He had learnt that a very elderly gentleman with the name of Mr A.J. Jephcott had died leaving property to his only living relative, a nephew who also was elderly and was living in Kennington, in south London. The nephew showed no interest, and on the advice of his solicitor, had immediately contacted an estate agent whose suggestion had been that the properties should be put up for auction. Tom had successfully bid and had become the owner of five cottages which were situated in the village of North Waltham. He was more than pleased with himself. He had great plans for these properties and intended to set a firm of local builders working on these buildings as soon as he could get home and discuss his plans with Sam.

Most folk would agree that when it came to grasping an opportunity Tom always seemed to have an uncanny foresight. For a few years now Tom had owned an enormous site in the East End of London where scrap metal was stored and processed until a suitable buyer was found. Since the war had ended he had travelled widely and called in a lot of favours. He had also used his connections with the Merchant Navy, which had gone a considerable way in his efforts to transport back to England heavily built vehicles, some armour plated, military jeeps and even tanks which had been abandoned in far flung corners of the world where fighting had taken place. And the beauty of it was, his business was one hundred per cent legal.

At the time, it was being said that the collection of so much abandoned scrap metal was not worth the effort needed and most of the authorities concerned were of the opinion that it was far easier just to write it off. Let it lie and rot.

Tom, with that wise head on such young shoulders, had had other ideas.

Showing great perseverance, he had finally been granted Government Permits, which enabled him to search for and retrieve all such scrap metal. Money makes money, as the saying goes, and it had certainly become a successful venture for Tom. And a very profitable one at that.

Emma was still laughing to herself as she rubbed the earth from her hands, picked up her bowl, now well filled with vegetables, and started back towards the house. Two sons-in-law, as different as chalk and cheese, and yet they seemed to get on so well when ever they were together. The way her two girls had suddenly settled on which man they wanted to spend the rest of their lives with was totally unbelievable. If she had planned it all herself she couldn't have done any better.

Emma allowed herself a smile, albeit a cynical one, at the same time saying to herself, 'Let's get these weddings over, and maybe the first ten years, and then I might begin to believe in happy-ever-after endings.'

# Twenty-One

Tom Yates had never been one for hanging about; he hit upon an idea and he acted on it. However, when he came home with Bella that weekend and told the family that he had obtained a special marriage licence and hopefully he and Bella would be able to get married within seven days if the Reverend Michael Coyle would agree to perform the ceremony, it certainly took the wind out of both Sam and Emma.

'Seven days? You mean next weekend?' Emma almost choked on the words.

'Why should we wait?' Tom asked, grinning from ear to ear. 'It's springtime and hopefully the weather will be good to us, and we'll be able to have an open air kind of wedding reception.'

'But it's so soon; none of us have anything to wear. And what about the invitations? There won't be time enough to get them all out. And have you given any thought to the food?'

'We'll get it announced over the local radio, let everyone know they will be welcome.' Tom had an answer for everything!

'Oh, Tom, you've been involved in some harebrained schemes in your time but this takes the biscuit, and no mistake.' Emma's tone of voice showed just how frantic she was feeling.

Sam was all for agreeing with her but somehow he had to let her know that it wasn't their decision. Emma was doing her best to concentrate on cutting slices of bread ready for toasting. If only everyone would sit down and begin to eat their breakfast it would give her some time to think.

It was Emma who produced a writing pad and two or three pencils at breakfast. When everyone stared at her she shrugged, 'If they are going to do it, let's all pitch in and make sure we do it right.'

'Terrific,' Tom said laughing and looking as pleased as Punch. 'As soon as we've finished eating Bella and I will go to see Reverend Coyle.' Then getting to his feet he wrapped his arms around the only mother he had ever known and gently kissed the top of her head.

'Mum, please, will you stop worrying? I do so want it to be a happy day. As for the food, I know there will be ample local produce for the evening party but for our family do, the main meal, the three-tier cake and all the trimmings, I have already arranged for it all to be brought down from London. A firm of caterers will be responsible for the whole caboodle, and that includes the staff. I have also cleared it with Richard; he offered, and I've accepted, that the wedding breakfast, just family and close friends, is to be held up at the Big House. You will be the mother of the bride, it will be your big day, and Bella wants you to enjoy it just as much as I do. So, am I going to be allowed to go ahead and make sure that I have Bella for my wife?'

'Tom! There are times when I could cheerfully murder you yet you have such a knack of getting round everybody. Right now I have the feeling that the next seven days are going to be a bit hectic.' Having said that she glanced across to where Sam was standing with an arm around each of his daughters. He raised his eyebrows at her and mouthed, 'You can say that again.'

It was unusual for Sam Pearson to feel that he was out of his depth but this morning he had sighed heavily and told himself there had to be a first time for everything. What with Emma dragging him off to the shops demanding that he be rigged out from top to toe, and now Tom asking him to get involved in the refurbishment of these five cottages he had bought, it was all getting a bit too much.

'I'm not asking you to do any of the actual work, Sam, just be the site manager – you know what I mean, put in an appearance when the tradesmen least expect you, keep them on their toes, and see that the tenants are given every consideration while the work is going on.'

'That's all very well, son, but these people have lived in that row of cottages most of their lives and they are terrified that when all the modern plumbing and other renovations which you have planned are completed they will either be asked to pay more rent than they can afford, or they'll be given notice to quit. And by the way, I've been meaning to have a word with you – you do know Aggie, her two lads and Mary live in the last cottage, don't you?'

'Of course I do,' Tom's grin was both sly and cunning.

'You haven't let on to her that you are the new owner; you've let her agonize over what is going to happen, and it doesn't seem all that fair. Aggie's been good to you in the past.'

Tom looked at his watch and then glanced up the road. 'Ah, bang on cue. Let's not split hairs, Sam, Aunt Agnes is coming towards us now, so let's hear what she's got to say.'

Both men turned to face Aggie. She looked shocked and bewildered and the first words she spat out certainly proved that her feelings were mixed. She was still a few feet away when she let fly. 'You, Tom Yates, you're deeper than any ocean, and I for one am going to have to give up trying to get to the bottom of you. Been to the solicitors, I have, but you know all about that, don't you? This last half-hour I've gone from wanting to kill you with my bare hands to loving you even more than I always have done, if that's possible. Oh, Tom, what am I going to do about you?'

Tom was looking self-conscious, standing first on one foot and then on the other, not knowing what to say, which was a first for him.

Sam looked from one to the other and roared, 'Will someone please tell me what is going on?'

Aggie undid the clasp on her handbag and took out a large envelope from which she withdrew a legal looking document. Holding it out to Sam, she cleared her throat, yet her words were little more than a whisper as she said, 'These are the deeds to my cottage. The solicitor tells me I now own the property outright, no rent to pay ever again. It seems that Tom has given me my cottage, it's ... it's just too, too much.' And with that she burst into a flood of tears.

Tom put his arms around her ample body and held her close, her face resting against his broad chest. She was still protesting, 'It's all too much.'

'Aunt Agnes, will you listen to me for a minute, please? It's my way of saying thanks to you for being there all those years ago when John and I turned up with nothing but what we stood up in. Just think of it as pay-back time. And by the way, you must take those deeds to the bank for safe keeping.'

Aggie brushed her hand across her wet cheeks. 'That's what the solicitor advised but I told him, same as I'm telling you, not until tomorrow. I'm going to sit and look at them all afternoon and later I'll show them to Sid, Len and Mary, let them know what this means. But Tom, lad, I still say you shouldn't, it's far too much.'

With the evening before the actual wedding

came a bit of peace, and Emma and Sam were alone in the house. 'Sam,' Emma broke the silence. 'Have you any idea where they are going to live?'

'By *they*, I take it that you are referring to our Bella and Tom,' Sam queried, as he folded the evening newspaper he had been reading. 'All I know is what Tom told both of us, that Jack Briggs had offered to sell him a few acres of his land and that Tom has accepted and has already applied to the Council for building permission.'

'I know all that; Tom even showed me the plans he has had drawn up for a four-bedroom house. But all of that has got to be in the distant future. What I was asking about is the here and now. This time tomorrow our Bella will be Mrs Yates.'

'Emma, you are pleased about that, aren't you? Thought we agreed, those two are made for each other.'

'You know darn well I'm over the moon about both our girls. I just wanted to know what was happening about living quarters after tomorrow.'

'I'll ask Tom later if I get a chance to get him on his own, but now I come to think about it – didn't you tell me that Joyce Briggs had offered to rent them one of those holiday places they've got up at the farm, just as a stop-gap?'

'Maybe. I don't remember, there's been so much going on. Tom will have it sorted though, won't he?'

'Of course he will,' Sam said, getting to his feet and managing to smile. This last week their whole lives had been up-turned. 'I think we should go to bed now, get some sleep. As the mother of the bride you want to look your best tomorrow.'

'Good idea,' Emma said, holding out her hand to him.

Hand in hand they made for the stairs, only pausing for Sam to close the kitchen door quietly behind them.

Sam heard voices and much laughter as he rubbed his hand groggily over his face. Beside him Emma struggled to sit up.

'What the hell is going on?' It's Bella's wedding day, she suddenly realized as she quickly swung her legs over the side of the bed. Sam was already standing at the window and his shoulders were shaking with laughter. 'Just look at them, it's barely six o'clock and they're doing their best to wake the whole neighbourhood up.'

Sid, Len and Mary Brownlow seemed to

be the ringleaders yet there were many other lads and lasses all armed with cardboard boxes, all talking in loud whispers and doing their best to muffle their laughter.

'What's going on?' Emma demanded to know, as Sam opened the window and she was able to lean out.

'We're decorating your street, Aunt Em. Bella will have to walk to the corner because the wedding car won't be able to drive down and we thought we'd pretty the cobbles up a bit.' Lenny lifted a large box and tilted it upwards for Emma to see the contents – heaps of balloons, silver bells, rolls and rolls of white and silver paper.

Despite her better judgement, Emma was thrilled. To think that all the local youngsters were getting themselves involved in her Bella's wedding day really was a very nice gesture, yet she winced as she watched two lads scuttle up a tree to twine decorations from the branches.

'What's going on, Mum?' Bella chuckled as she came into her parents' bedroom and crossed over to look out of the window. Her father gathered her tight in his arms. 'Last chance I shall get to cuddle my daughter.' He was pretending to be sad, yet his voice was filled with laughter as they watched the antics going on down below in the street.

Emily too had been woken by the noise and she thought the goings-on were hilarious, yet it was she that took control. 'We've got to decide who is going to hog the tin bath first because you and I, my dear sister, are going to need more than one hour to make ourselves beautiful. You too, Mum, you've some primping to do. Anyway, I'm going to put the kettle on, as there won't be many cups of tea flying around today; if I know Tom it will be champagne all the way.'

Emma's nerves seemed to have transferred to her elder daughter. While the bride calmly dressed for her wedding, it was Emily that fussed with the flowers and the buttonholes, and paced from window to front door looking for the photographer.

'He should have been here a quarter of an hour ago,' she muttered. 'I want to make sure that he takes a few shots of just Bella with our dad.' She turned, breaking off what she'd been saying to Mary, who was to be the second bridesmaid, when she saw her mother coming down the stairs.

'Oh. You look really beautiful, Mum, you couldn't have chosen better.'

Emma was wearing a soft beige silk calf length dress with only a touch of ecru lace around the neck, the hem and on the cuffs of the long sleeves. The sales lady's advice had been good. She had persuaded Emma to buy a matching picture hat and Bella had shown her mother how to fluff her hair out under the brim.

Bella gave a slight cough to draw attention to herself as she appeared at the top of the stairs.

Emily turned and her gasp was one of utter surprise. She had helped her sister to dress but had come downstairs before Bella had put the final touches.

'Emily, you don't think this head dress is too much, do you?'

Bella reached up, her fingers fiddling with the pearls that were twined around tiny white rosebuds.

'Bella, my darling sister, you look absolutely fantastic!'

It was no exaggeration. The white sheaf of a dress looked as if Bella had been poured into it. Yet the style was so simple, simply cut, simply beautiful. Perfection personified!

Tears of joy were shining in Bella's eyes and her mother thought it time that she spoke up. 'My love, you look as a bride should look, absolutely glowing. I'm sure your father will cry when he sees you but I must not shed one tear because, even with your help and Emily's advice, I spent forever on my make-up.'

She turned to give her eldest daughter and Mary Brownlow the once-over and again she was lost for words. The floor-length dresses chosen for the bridesmaids were the palest blue silk with leg-o'-mutton sleeves and a row of twelve pearl buttons reaching from the elbow down to the wrist. High-heeled silver sandals gave the finishing touch.

'How did we ever manage to get all these fineries together in such a short time? I could have murdered our Tom when he first told us he and Bella were getting married within seven days, but now look at all of you!' Emma shook her head quickly.

'Mum, you're not going to cry,' Bella said, touching her mother's arm.

'None of us are going to cry,' Emily said firmly. 'The photographer is just coming down the road, so are we all ready?'

'I wonder how Tom got on, staying with Richard up at the Big House last night?' Bella grinned, as they all made their way toward the front of the house.

Emily met her sister's eyes and they both burst out laughing. 'I'd have given a lot to have been a fly on the wall. It's a wonder our ears weren't burning like mad,' Bella said thoughtfully.

It was their mother who was suddenly saying, 'Something old, something new, something borrowed and something blue – have you girls given a thought to the old superstition?'

Colour rose in Bella's cheeks and Emily smiled widely. 'Yes, we have,' they said in agreement. 'Start at the top,' Emily advised.

'All right,' Bella turned to face her mother and lifted a hand to touch her head dress. 'Mum, you said you wore this string of pearls the day you married Dad, so that's something old. My dress is new and my underwear is trimmed with blue silk ribbons.'

Emma reached out and touched her youngest daughter's cheek. She felt a great impulse to take her in her arms and hug her tightly. Instead she resisted the temptation and stepped back. 'Well, I suppose that only leaves something borrowed.'

Both girls giggled. Emily nodded her head, then Bella leant forward, and with both hands she lifted the hem of her wedding dress until it was well above her knees. On display was a garter, the colour was bright red and it was interwoven with strands of black satin ribbon. The silence lasted a full thirty seconds, after which it would have been hard to tell which female was laughing the most uproariously.

'Emily lent it to me,' Bella managed to mutter.

'I guessed that much. Being in the army has certainly widened her horizons,' their mother said, as they heard their father calling them to say the photographer was waiting. Shaking her head, Emma led the way, doing her best to conceal her amusement. That garter is going to see daylight a few times today, I'll be bound, but not before the wedding ceremony is over, I hope, she was furtively saying to herself.

Sam took one look at his wife and daughters and he was choked.

'My bevy of beauties!' was all that he was able to stammer.

The camera snapped time and time again until someone shouted, 'The cars are here.'

'Bella, are you ready?' her father asked, offering his arm.

'Yes.' Yet she looked at her mother and then looked back at the house in which she had been born, and groped for her mother's hand. Then, holding firmly on to her father, she walked along the cobbles to where the chauffeur was holding open the door of the car. A great cheer went up from the neighbours as the first car holding the Brownlow family moved off, then the second car which was ferrying the two bridesmaids, her sister Emily and Mary Brownlow.

'I'm going to drive you, sir, and the bride around the lanes for about ten minutes,' the chauffeur explained to Sam. 'Wouldn't do for the bride to arrive first.'

A pin, if dropped, could have been heard as the bride, on her father's arm, appeared in the doorway of the church. Sam looked at his daughter and smiled fondly, then he walked her down the aisle to stand beside Tom.

'Dearly beloved,' the Reverend Michael Coyle began.

Emma did cry, so did Aggie, and they weren't alone.

'I now pronounce you husband and wife.'

Then the rafters of Saint Michael's church echoed as the organist burst into the opening bars of the Wedding March.

A cheer went up from outside the church where so many people had gathered. Sam wasn't the least bit surprised to see a charabanc parked alongside the grass verge. Tom's friends from the East End of London were not going to be left out of today's celebrations!

The camera was brought back into operation. 'One with the parents, please.' There were whistles and shouts as Sam explained he and Emma were like parents to both the bride and the groom!

'Nice one.' Tom grinned as he threw his arms around Sam. 'Father and father-in-law.'

'Come on, Tom, there's still loads of folk who wish to take pictures.' Emma plucked Tom from Sam's arms. 'Give your mother-in-law a kiss.'

'Mum,' he whispered. 'I have so much to thank you for. I've had you for my mum since I was nine years old, thank God.'

The official reception was held in the main dining room of the Big House. Lionel and Marion were seated with the family on the top table.

'We'll be doing it all again come the autumn,' Marion said to her son.

'Indeed we shall,' Richard agreed, smiling as he squeezed Emily's hand.

This wonderful, wonderful day passed so quickly and then it was evening. Fires were lit, and everywhere you turned food was being cooked. The whole village had turned out.

'We never saw you kiss the bride,' Daisy Gaskin teased Tom.

'Oh, if that's all that's bothering you we'll soon put things to rights,' Tom quickly retorted. Even as he was chuckling, he took his wife into his arms and gently covered her mouth with his own, letting the kiss linger, deepening it, until Bella forgot that they were standing in a field surrounded by people. And so did Tom!

'Let that girl go and behave yourself, Tom Yates.' Kate Simmons, chairwoman of the Women's Guild and a friend of Emma, shook her head at the pair of them. 'You should be mingling with your guests. If you want to smooch you just wait until later. You never did have much common sense.'

'Yes, ma'am! Sorry, ma'am.' Tom was doing his best to keep a straight face.

'Right from a nipper he's always been a bit of a tearaway, so he has.' Kate winked at Daisy.

'You don't 'ave t'tell me about him,' Daisy retorted laughing. 'But you have to agree, he's a handsome-so-and-so.'

'They're both right.' Bella tossed back her

hair and gave Tom a long, teasing look.

'What? You're agreeing that you are very lucky to have married such a handsome bloke?'

'No, I'm not,' Bella chuckled. 'I'm agreeing with Kate, that you never did have any common sense.'

Tom had to have the last word. 'Bella, my darling, it's not long since you promised to love, honour and obey me.'

The fireworks had all been lit, most of the food had been eaten, and the bonfires were burning low as, hand-in-hand, Bella and Tom came to find their parents.

'We're going to slip away but we wanted to say thanks for everything.' For once in his life Tom looked embarrassed.

Emma stepped closer to them and put her arms around them both. 'Always take care of each other,' she murmured and then softly she added, 'I thank God for this day!'

Sam lingered over his hugging of Bella; this was his youngest daughter.

'I know you will both be fine,' he managed to utter. Then, with his wife held tightly by his side, he watched as, with their hands joined, Mr and Mrs Yates walked across the grass together.

# Twenty-Two

The months of summer had given them long, lovely hot days with so much activity going on in the village of North Waltham that most folk could be forgiven if the terrors of the Second World War had been laid aside. Not forgotten, but no longer daily remembered. Now there was time for happiness and looking forward to the future. In particular, Emma Pearson felt this was very much the situation with her family. There never seemed to be a dull moment these days and although she often worried herself sick because there were so many tasks she had set herself for this coming autumn, if the truth be known she wouldn't have had it any other way. In fact, as she allowed her thoughts to run back over the last four months her heart bubbled with excitement.

'Hey, Mum, what are you doing still digging about out here?' Emily called out cheerily as she came round the side of the house and joined her mother. 'Tomatoes are looking good and there are still plenty of vegetables. Still taking care of this plot yourself, are you? We can always get a gardener to give you a hand. You've only got to say.'

Her eldest daughter turning up unexpectedly brought a smile to Emma's face, but she hastily asked, 'Are you suggesting that I'm past doing a bit to me own garden? Because if you are, let me tell you I enjoy pottering about out here.'

'Would I so much as dare to suggest any such thing?' Emily smiled at her mother as she put her arm around her and planted a kiss on her rosy cheek.

'All right then, I forgive you. Have you got time to come into the house and have a cup of tea or coffee before you race away again?'

'Of course, I have. I haven't just popped in, there are several things I need to go over with you. I'll go indoors and put the kettle on while you finish off here.'

Emma stood watching the retreating back of her eldest daughter and her forehead was creased into a deep frown. She couldn't stop herself from being concerned. Both Bella and Emily were so dear to her and there wasn't anything in this world that she would not do for either one of them. Nowadays it was a relief to know how happy and settled Bella and Tom were, even though Tom was doing his best to change a good many things in this small village. Not that it bothered the local people; most praised Tom to the hilt and to some Tom could do no wrong. The work on the five cottages he had purchased was finished a long time ago and the tenants never tired of showing other folk around their improved homes and equally never tired of emphasizing the fact that Tom had not increased their weekly rent. And Bella was still happy as a pig in muck, still offering to give a hand on Jack Briggs' farm whenever they were short-handed. Though Emma was inclined to believe that Bella was living for the day when she and Tom would be able to move into their four-bedroom house. To herself and Sam it was incredible that Tom had managed to work so many wonders. A newly-built house, standing in its own grounds! God knows how he had achieved so much, yet he himself hadn't altered, not one iota! He was, underneath all the good clothes he could afford these days, still the lovable, kind-hearted lad that had landed on their doorstep all those years ago. No, it wasn't that pair that she worried over – it was Emily and Richard.

Emily's time in the army had changed her, changed her into someone every different. She had grown up, that was for sure. She was totally confident, hard, and strong in all the ways that Bella wasn't. Yet both girls could show softness and kindness when it suited them. It wasn't that Bella was boring, far from it. She was a character full of spice and gumption. Emma knew the word she was avoiding when thinking about Emily – aside from being so truly beautiful, she was downright sexy. Emma wasn't even sure if her eldest daughter herself was aware of that fact.

Richard had suggested that Emily did not take on any paid employment and it was true to say there was so much work that Emily had to oversee in the Big House whilst Richard was winding up his affairs in London that it did not give her very much free time.

Some weeks, though, Emily would go back to London with Richard and stay with him at his apartment until such time as he was free to come back to North Waltham. This kind of cohabitation did not meet with Sam's approval and Emma too often thought she would feel much more contented when Richard and their Emily were legally married.

It was after Emily had been in London for a spell that, on her return, she would be full of wicked little stories about well-known famous people. Who had said what, who had lovers despite the fact that the couple involved were supposedly happily married to other people. Listening to her sometimes, Emma was troubled that all this high life might change her. For all that, she and Sam couldn't help but be impressed by the way their daughter was coping with what was, in truth, a totally different life.

The last Saturday in October finally arrived. The day that Emily Pearson would become the wife of Richard Trenfield.

From the moment Sam woke his wife up by coming into their bedroom bearing a tray of tea, and during the short period while they sat side by side on the edge of their bed, Emma was under no illusion. This wedding day would bear no resemblance whatsoever to Bella and Tom's!

The ceremony was to be held in the same church, also officiated by the Reverend Michael Coyle. The wedding breakfast again was to be set out in the main dining hall up at the Big House. But there the comparison ended. Today everything would be perfect.

Really perfect.

Somehow Emma got herself ready and as she reached up to straighten the knot in the dark blue tie Sam was wearing with a dark grey suit, she sadly said, 'I'm missing our Emily not going from here. It seems as if we are going to a friend's wedding rather than to our own daughter's.'

'Oh Lord, Em, don't start all that again now. Emily has gone over and over it a dozen times. All her things including her bridal wear are all up at the hall. It made sense to go to the church from there. Bella is up there; you know she is Matron of Honour and she is seeing to the three bridesmaids. Can't you let it be?' Sam's voice held a strong note of pleading and Emma quickly apologized.

'I know I'm being petty, but I'm feeling a bit left out of everything, if you want me to be honest. I'll be all right once we get to the church.'

'Well, our car should be here any minute. Richard said he was sending one just for you and me as parents of the bride, but I shall leave you with Tom as soon as Emily arrives at the church because I am still walking my daughter up the aisle.'

'Who are the other cars for?'

'I don't think Richard is sending more cars. I understand it is to be two horse-drawn open carriages, one for Aggie and her brood and the other one for the use of any of our near neighbours. I thought that was right thoughtful of Richard.'

'Yes, it is. Sorry, Sam, didn't mean t'get meself all rattled.'

'No need to worry, my love, I know exactly what is eating away at you.'

'You do? Well perhaps you had better tell me.'

'After today all our chicks will have left the nest and you are feeling a bit lost. But look on the bright side; I'll lay a bet with you now that we'll be grandparents in the not too distant future. How will that suit you?'

Emma's face broke into a broad beam and her voice was a whole lot more cheerful as she said, 'Oh, Sam, wouldn't it be great?'

'I think I can safely say that I have just laid a bet with you, Emma, so will you please come outside and wait for the various forms of transport to arrive and show the neighbours your new outfit, which has cost me a fortune because you said you couldn't be photographed in the same outfit at both our girls' weddings.'

Sam ducked as he spoke, which was lucky,

because Emma had just swung her new handbag at him.

For the whole of the morning Marion Trenfield had contrived to keep her son away from the part of the house where the bride-to-be, the bridesmaids were, and God alone knew how many dressers and hair stylists it needed to make this bevy of young ladies look beautiful.

Now she leaned back, wriggled her shoulders into the soft leather upholstery of the limousine, reached for her husband's hand and, as the car slowly swept through the gates of the Big House on its way to the church, she finally allowed herself to softly breathe out.

'Are you all right?' Lionel gently asked, squeezing the hand she had placed in to his.

'I am now, but oh my dearest, I shall be glad when Michael finally announces that Richard and Emily are man and wife. Many more days like the past few and I think I would be in danger of falling apart.'

Lionel waggled their hands and laughed. 'Not you, my darling, you are made of sterner stuff. However, I do agree we must have been near to reaching breaking point. But never mind, the hour is about to dawn and from this moment we are going to enjoy the fact that we are gaining a lovely daughter and we are both certain of just how happy Richard is.' Having finished his short speech, Lionel let go of his wife's hand, leaned forward and rapped on the glass partition that separated the passengers from the driver.

'Yes, sir?' the driver spoke into the mouthpiece that was on the dashboard.

'Are we running early? What I mean is, do we have a little time to spare?' Lionel quietly enquired.

'We certainly are early, sir. Would you like me to drive around the lanes rather than you and your lady wife sit in the church pews for any length of time?'

'Not exactly, driver. What I would like you to do is to find a safe lay-by, anywhere as long as it is off the road, and you can park up safely for just a short while.'

'Right sir, I've got your meaning.' And within minutes the driver was steering the big car across a grassy verge and bringing it to a halt below the branches of a big leafy oak tree.

Lionel lost no time; from beneath the seat he produced a small wicker wine basket and on opening the lid Marion gasped but immediately said aloud, 'Why am I not surprised? This gesture is so like you, Lionel, and I must say I do appreciate your thoughtfulness.'

With monogrammed linen serviettes spread across their knees Lionel made a great show of opening a bottle of champagne and pouring some into two crystal cut glasses. Raising his glass he looked into his wife's eyes and held her gaze for a minute before saying, 'Darling, thank you for having given me three sons. God saw fit to take two of them when still in the prime of their lives, but today you are the mother of the bridegroom and no man on this earth ever had a more wonderful mother. So my first toast is to you, Marion, as Richard's mother.'

They each raised their glass and drank, yet everything in the car was a blur to Marion because her eyes were brimming with tears.

Lionel wasn't finished. 'Listen carefully, my love,' he murmured, 'this toast is a selfish one, it is all about me. How healthy I am, how successful I have been in my life, what a wonderful house and home I have had for many years and what a marvellous woman I have had by my side all these years to help steer me in the right direction. But most important of all, how loving and caring that woman has been from the very first day that I set eyes on her. Marion, I haven't words to tell you how much you mean to me. Thank you for all the years we have had together and please God we still have a few more to go.'

In silence they sipped from their glasses until Lionel took both glasses and set them down on to the seat beside him. He now gazed at his wife and his thoughts were telling him that seldom had she looked more lovely.

She was dressed in a dark blue velvet gown, which fell in graceful folds to touch the tip of her blue leather shoes. Around her shoulders lay a large cloak, the material of which was also a rich velvet yet the colour was a deep dark shade of red, and lying on the seat beside her was a pair of elbow-length soft leather gloves in the same shade of red. His eyes were suddenly glazed in admiration yet all he could utter was, 'You are still so beautiful, Marion.'

'You're looking pretty chirpy yourself,' Marion was quick to assure him, and so he was. His full head of white hair had been cut and brushed by the local barber that very morning and his moustache had been trimmed. Naturally his morning suit was immaculate and his not-forgotten waistcoat defied any criticism. It was white silk embellished with gold buttons as befitted the father of the groom!

Marion held out her hand and Lionel clasped it, and only then did he take his wife into his arms and hold her close.

It was a while before his lips covered hers in a soft lingering kiss. No more words were necessary; still with his arms around his wife Lionel called out, 'All right, driver, we've a wedding to attend so I think we had better be making a move.'

The driver, who had done his best to slide down in his seat so as not to appear too intrusive but had been more moved than he would have liked to admit, quickly straightened his peaked cap and said, 'Right, sir, to the church now, is it?'

It was Marion Trenfield that answered. 'Yes, please, driver.'

Her husband was too busy trying to keep his emotions in check. As the car slowly moved back on to the roadway, Marion and Lionel leaned back against the leather upholstery.

'Are you all right, my love?' Lionel softly asked his wife.

Marion nodded.

They both sighed, and sounded as contented as any pair of young lovers might.

The church was filled with well-dressed people, but, somehow, it was Richard who was drawing the interested, admiring glances as he waited at the altar for his bride to arrive. He looked splendid in his well-cut morning suit, yet to those that were close to him there was an air of vulnerability about him. His hair was glossy but his bright eyes were showing a mixture of emotions and he was thinking to himself that it was a good job that it was impossible for the guests to read his thoughts.

He had fallen in love with a girl quite a few years younger than himself. A girl he had known almost from the day she had been born, and yet he continually asked himself: just how well did he know her? She could be passionate, but reserved at times. She was competent, her wartime service had proved that. She was a mixture of so many things, a tantalizing mystery waiting to be solved. Perhaps that was why he loved her so much. Could she really love him as much as he loved her? Oh, how he hoped and prayed that it was so.

Suddenly there was quite a stir amongst

the congregation. The bride had arrived on the arm of her father and many females were gasping at the sight of the bride-to-be gliding gracefully towards her groom.

'You look so beautiful,' Richard said as she took her place beside him.

As the strains of the wedding march died away, the Reverend Coyle began, 'Dearly beloved, we are gathered here today...'

They promised to forsake all others and finally the Reverend asked 'Do you, Emily Amelia Pearson, take Richard Alistair Trenfield to be your lawful wedded husband?'

Sitting in the front pew Emma was holding on tightly to Sam's hand and crying softly but at the same time thinking how wonderful it all was. Even their names had a special ring to them.

Michael Coyle pronounced them man and wife and they, with both sets of parents, proceeded to the back of the church to sign the register.

In the grounds of the church it seemed as if every inhabitant of the village had come to watch. They threw confetti and several small children approached to shyly give Emily and Richard silver horse-shoes and cards that wished them a long and happy life together.

It was a happy time, a happy day, but as

Emma reminded Sam, it was far from being over yet.

The wedding breakfast was a great success. Toasts had been drunk and speeches made and now the people who knew and loved Emily were kissing her and wishing her and Richard a wonderful future. 'I love you so much,' Richard told her whenever he got the opportunity. 'I love you too,' she kept whispering back.

As more guests arrived, Richard couldn't take his eyes off his beautiful wife. She was being so gracious. She moved easily among the guests, talked to a few of the men she had become acquainted with whilst staying in London and then, with Bella by her side, spent time with the women, some of whom they had grown up with. The two sisters finally sought out Marion and Lionel Trenfield who were seated at a side table having a drink with Emma and Sam Pearson. Emily bent her head and, moving from one mother to the other, she kissed the cheeks of both women, asking if they were all right and if she could get them anything.

'We are absolutely fine,' Marion replied quickly. 'This is your day, go and enjoy it.' Before Emily was given a chance to answer, the band struck up a slow dreamy waltz and Lionel got to his feet. Holding his arms wide he smiled broadly and asked, 'May I please have this dance with my daughter-in-law?'

They began to slowly dance around the floor. Almost everyone got to their feet and stood staring in admiration. Lionel, who seemed quite overcome by emotion, guided her easily around the floor until the second time he drew her level with her father, when he stopped. 'Time you took over, Sam, you're a helluva lot younger than I,' he said, releasing his hold on Emily and sliding down to sit beside his wife.

'Oh, Dad, how can I thank you and Mum and everyone else? It has been such a special day.'

'No thanks are needed, not to anyone; just make sure you and Richard have a truly good life.' He tightened his hold on his daughter, and as the band quickened the music slightly, he showed the audience that the father of the bride was not too old to show off on the dance floor. All these goings-on had both Marion and Emma really amus-ed.

Tom had joined Richard; together they watched the two sisters mingle and they were in agreement. It had been a truly wonderful day, great food, interesting people, lively conversations and so much true love it was unbelievable.

Even the weather had been kind, the sunshine emphasizing the glorious autumn colours of the trees and the shrubs which hopefully would show to advantage in all the photographs that had been taken.

Then, at last, it was time for the happy couple to leave. They had been upstairs to change, and Emily was wearing a navy blue suit with a crisp white blouse as she stood on the stage with the band, and turned her back to the crowd, and threw her bouquet high above and behind her. It flew through the air and landed in the arms of Mary Brownlow who immediately buried her face in the blooms. It did not escape her mother's notice that a tall lad who worked for Barclays Bank and had been calling at their house several times recently was giving the thumbs-up sign to her daughter!

Despite the numerous questions as to where the happy couple were going on honeymoon, not one soul had received a straight answer. That was because their destination was Richard's apartment in London. It had been a mutual decision. Privacy was what they were after!

Emily had kissed her parents and Richard had kissed his mother and assured his father that they would only be away for fourteen days. 'Be good, you two,' Emily said to Tom and Bella as she hugged them both before she got into the car, and as Richard drove away, Tom pulled his wife into his arms and kissed her.

'Great day; everything went so well,' Bella remarked as she snuggled more tightly into Tom's arms.

'Yeah, great to have a family, especially one such as ours.' Tom's voice was soft but he had never sounded more serious in the whole of his life.

Bella needed no telling what he was thinking of or just how appreciative he always felt. Now it was Bella that covered Tom's lips with her own and she kissed him with a passion that certainly matched his. He might have come into her life as a brother but before she was even out of her teenage years she had known he was destined to be her husband. For three weeks now she had been aware that she was pregnant, but, not wanting to steal the thunder away from her sister on her wedding day, she had told no one except her mother. She had forbidden her mother to even let on to her father.

Reluctantly Emma had agreed, even though it had been a hard battle to keep such news to herself.

Looking around Bella saw that her mother was standing alone and had been watching her and Tom. 'Time to go; come with me to say goodnight to Mum and Dad,' Bella said. Loosening herself from her husband's arms she grasped his hand and together they walked across the room.

Emma had started to get nervous. She had for days and nights longed to tell Sam that he had been right because soon Bella would be giving them their first grandchild. How much harder must it have been for Bella to hold her secret close? Now tonight she felt sure Bella would tell Tom. That young man would be over the moon, that was a fact of which she was one hundred per cent certain.

'Goodnight, Mum. Where's Dad?' Bella asked, glancing round the room.

'He and Lionel have gone off to have a quiet nightcap; I'll tell him you said goodnight and that you will see him in the morning.'

Tom had his back to them, he was shaking hands with a couple who were leaving. Emma smiled at her youngest daughter and pretended to clap her hands silently. 'You come down and tell your father. I still won't say a word.' Emma was whispering, then she giggled nervously. 'But first you have to find the right moment to tell Tom.'

'Oh, Mum, I honestly don't know how I have managed to keep the news from him for so long, but I was right to do so, I'm sure I was. It wouldn't have been fair with everyone excited about Emily's wedding.'

'All right, Mrs Yates, let's go, time we were in bed,' Tom said to Bella as he crept up on them and bent low in order to kiss his mother-cum-mother-in-law good-night.

Hand in hand they walked down the lanes and across the fields to the holiday chalet that Tom had been renting from Jack Briggs. Once inside, Bella went straight to the bathroom, brushed her teeth and washed her hands and face, and put on her nightgown. Tom was already in bed when she came into the room and she slipped into bed beside him. They had both had more than enough to drink today so Tom just wrapped her in his arms, ready to hold her until they both fell asleep.

'How long before our house will be ready for us to move into?'

Tom was a bit shaken. The tone of Bella's voice as she had asked the question had been sharp.

'Funny question for this time of night,' he declared, showing that he was a bit put out by it.

'No, it's not. It is straightforward enough. How long?'

Tom pushed her aside and swung his legs over the side of the bed. 'Suddenly you don't like this place? Why the sudden rush to move?' Tom was worried. They had been up at the Big House all day, and Bella had seen all the alterations and refurbishments that Richard had had done. Had Bella been envious? Normally it wasn't like her, but then again she was a woman, and who knew what went on in their minds half the time?

But she was well aware of how hard he and the builders were striving to get their new house ready, so why suddenly make such a big thing of it and at this time of night when they were both tired?

Bella leaned towards him and stole a glance. She was worried now – had she been silly and pushed Tom too far?

'It would be nice if just our bedroom and a nursery were fit to use,' she said, sounding very timid.

It took a second or two before the penny dropped and Tom's head jerked up. 'Say that again!' he demanded, keeping a straight face, but with great difficulty.

'You heard me the first time. Care to tell me how long before I shall be able to start to decorate a nursery?'

It was some time before he turned his head towards her, and then he did it slowly as if he were afraid that she might be joking. She held out her hand, and he moved nearer to her but did not touch her. It was Bella who took his arm and dragged him backwards until she was able to lay his hand flat against her stomach. 'Not much of a swell yet but he or she will grow, I promise. I didn't want to tell anyone until after the wedding.'

Tom's eyes were brimming. He cleared his throat and chuckled. 'Actually, I don't know why I am so surprised – we haven't been able to get enough of each other from the day that Reverend Coyle announced that we were man and wife.'

'You're not mad that I kept it from you these past three weeks? I didn't want everyone making a fuss over me when it should be Emily's special time.'

Tom sat up and held out his arms to Bella. 'I love you, Bella, more than I thought it was possible for one person to love another. I spent the months leading up to our wedding thanking God that he had sent me to be part of the Pearson family. Think about it. From the day that Emma and Sam took John and me under their wing every single thing I have touched has turned out well. My life has not only turned around, it has become so unbelievable in so, so many ways. And you, my darling wife, will make the most wonderful mother in the whole world. I can't believe that you have kept the news all to yourself.'

'With so much going on I didn't think it was really the right time, but now…'

'You are a silly girl.' Tom took hold of Bella's hand and squeezed it, at the same time he gave her a questioning look.

'What is it, Tom? Is there something you want to ask me?'

'Yes.' He blurted the word out and then very quickly added, 'Please, if we 'ave a son, will you mind if we call him John?'

'You, my darling, are just a little bit late. From the moment I missed my period and then had a bout of morning sickness, I have been talking to him.' Bella paused and placed both of her hands flat across her belly. 'He knows he has to be a boy and that his name is John.'

'I'm that bloody thrilled,' Tom said. 'I

don't think either of us will get much sleep tonight but let's get back into bed and cuddle up.'

Bella's eyes sparkled as Tom held the bed-covers back, lifted her legs and made sure she was comfortable before he lay down beside her.

'I know we didn't plan this,' she said, 'but are you OK about it being so soon?'

Tom grinned. 'Who said we didn't plan it?' They lay quietly, hands loosely clasped and Tom was struggling to let his true feelings show. Suddenly he started to speak. 'I'm thinking how beautiful you will look while you're pregnant – oh, if only I could put into words what this means to me. I thought nothing could give me more joy than to have you for my wife, Bella, but now we'll be parents, I'll be a dad, and we'll 'ave our own family.'

His hold on her tightened, and he lifted her and drew her into his arms and began to kiss her with so much tenderness and passion that it was some minutes before either of them could bear to break away and even then he still kept her close within the circle of his arm as they snuggled down side by side.

Tom was muttering sleepily, 'We're going

to be a proper family with a great future ahead of us.'

Tom's words were few, yet he sounded so self assured. She gazed at him for a long moment. And then she smiled and it was a smile which had her face beaming with delight.

They lay in silence for a while, mulling over the fact that they were to have their first child, totally at ease with each other as they had always been since the day when Tom had first arrived in the village, a ragamuffin boy who believed that nobody wanted him.

Suddenly Tom sat up and took her hand in his. His voice was shaking with emotion as he said, 'It's been an amazing road I've travelled since your mum and dad took me under their wing, but if I've learned anything it is that family ties and family love mean more than any other thing in this whole world, and I am going to make sure that our children learn that fact real early on in their lives.'

'Tom, you said children! How do you know that we shall have more than one?' Bella said, teasing him.

Tom gave a really hearty laugh. 'I *know*, because I'm going to make sure that we do. I do love you, Bella, really love you, you and my own family is all I've ever wanted.'

Bella wasn't able to form an answer because Tom was kissing her.

And at that moment Bella felt she had never been happier.